THE LAST HERO

Fords of Nashville Series

USA Today **Bestselling Author**
HILDIE McQUEEN

Copyright Hildie McQueen © 2024
Print Edition

All rights reserved. No part of this book may be reproduced in any form or by any electronic or mechanical means—except in the case of brief quotations embodied in critical articles or reviews—without written permission.

Thank you for respecting the hard work of this author.

The characters and events portrayed in this book are fictitious. Any similarity to real persons, living or dead, is purely coincidental and not intended by the author

Also by Hildie McQueen
(In reading order)

<u>Fords of Nashville</u>
Even Heroes Cry
The Last Hero
Nobody's Hero

<u>Laurel Creek Trilogy</u>
Jaded: Luke
Broken: Taylor
Ruined: Tobias

<u>Other Works</u>
Montana Bachelor
Montana Beau
Montana Boss
Montana Bred
Montana Born
Melody of Secrets
Cowboy in Paradise

Chapter One

"**W**HY ARE YOU naked!" Cassie Tucker held up the tray of cupcakes and turned away from a very nude Jensen Ford. He sunbathed on a lounger behind the house where he'd been staying for the last few weeks while shooting a movie.

Cassie fought between taking a second look and keeping her eyes downcast. "Oh my God! I can't believe you're laying out here butt naked. Haven't you heard of a tanning bed?"

"Hello Cupcake Cassie." The actor's lips curved when she took another peek at him. Jensen was an arrogant ass who'd hurt her feelings multiple times…and he was over the top, unbelievably, amazingly hot.

Now she had a stunning vision burned into her brain, she'd never forget his well-toned tanned butt and long muscular legs. Admittedly, she didn't want to.

"For goodness sakes, you know people come and go through here all the time." Cassie took a step forward but feared tripping since she kept her face turned away to keep from gawking.

"Everyone's off set. They're filming in town today. I've got the afternoon off." His smooth deep voice flowed over her, and she glanced in his direction hoping he'd covered up.

He hadn't.

The egotistical jerk lifted up to his elbows and watched her with an amused grin.

"Can you cover up please?" Cassie snapped and rolled her eyes. "You are well aware I bring dessert over here in the afternoons. You're doing this on purpose. Put on some shorts or something."

"Can't."

"Why?" She stomped her foot immediately regretting the childish reaction. Jensen loved getting reactions out of people. The pompous ass knew just the right buttons to push to make her angry.

"Because I have a butt scene coming up and need an even tan." It sounded like he chuckled, but she couldn't be sure. "Just take those over to the hut and drop them off. You don't have to look at me."

Right. As if any woman who walked the planet could keep from taking in the sight of the "sexiest man alive's" totally bare body. Even when dressed he was a feast for the eyes. Nude on display, he was like an overdose of chocolate, if that existed. She sneaked another peek and immediately looked away.

Cassie kept her eyes on the door to the bistro-like hut that was built especially for the film crew in the back yard of the house treading carefully past where Jensen lay.

"Where is Chef?"

"Dunno."

She looked to the back of the house. Maybe the chef had gone inside to work in the larger kitchen. Not that it mattered where she left dessert, but if she left them outside there was a possibility they'd melt before Chef found them. On the other hand, to go in search of the man meant she'd have to go around Jensen. The still very naked Jensen.

The house was an old Victorian, which had been restored by Jensen's older brother Adam. The actor had sold the idea of his new movie location to the filming company. And now the movie "The Last Hero" was set to be the next summer's blockbuster.

Although the movie actors and film crew were a big boost for the economy of her small hometown, Lovely, Tennessee, it was also disruption to the otherwise quiet life the locals had grown used to.

Cassie couldn't complain, business had more than doubled at her small cupcake shop, *Sweet Indulgence*. Her second job, serving breakfast and lunch to the crew had also upped her income as well. Money that would help purchase a newer car. Her twelve-year-old Kia SUV was on the last leg of its last leg.

The tray was getting heavy. In the end she decided it was best to leave the cupcakes at the hut. It was cool enough under the overhang and the cakes were well protected in the box.

"Can I have one?" Jensen called out. He asked her the same thing every day. Each time it felt as if he did it to remind her of her place. That Cassie was much lower on the food chain that he was. As if she needed the reminder. Just looking at the expensive cars, exquisite clothes and even the fragrances worn by the wealthy people that accompanied him was a constant reminder of the difference in their social statuses.

In all fairness, Jensen Ford did not put off the same vibe as the other actors and the director team. He wore black jeans and t-shirts most days, his motorcycle boots were scuffed up and he rode an old Harley more than he did the sleek Jaguar parked next door at her friend Tesha's house.

"I won't bring you a cupcake if you don't cover up."

There was some grumbling and shifting. "Okay, I'm decent." He stood right behind her and Cassie jumped at the sound of his deep voice so close behind her left ear.

No way would she ever let him know how uncomfortable it made her. "Lemon or caramel?" She knew he'd pick the caramel. It was his favorite.

"Caramel please." His breath tickled the back of her neck, and she took a fortifying breath to keep from elbowing him and give the hint to move back. Thankfully her hands remained steady as she lifted an Ooey Gooey Caramel cupcake and placed it on the dessert plate. She put a fork next to it, a cloth napkin under the plate and turned to face him.

His hazel eyes met hers and she could see specks of gold and brown in them. His lashes were thick and long when he looked down to the dessert.

When he didn't lift his hands to take it, Cassie shoved it into this chest. Unfortunately that meant she had to notice how well formed and broad it was. Her gaze traveled down to his flat stomach and the edge of a towel he'd wrapped around his waist.

"Why are you still mad at me?" Jensen asked, still not taking the cupcake. "I apologized." His lopsided grin made her stomach flip. Damn him for being so damn good-looking.

Cassie snapped out of her ogling and pretended interest in the landscape behind him. "It wasn't much of an apology. And I accepted it. I am not mad at you, I don't hold grudges."

"Right."

A couple weeks earlier, Jensen had apologized for making a comment about how he didn't think a cupcake business was to be taken seriously. Tesha, her friend and Jensen's soon to be sister-in-law made him apologize.

In the middle of his apology, he'd insulted her again by stating, "I just don't think a smart person would open a specialty shop in such a small town and expect to earn a living."

"But you continue to act angry."

Why did he insist on this conversation? All she wanted was to drop off the cupcakes and leave. Had tried to ensure no interruptions, not running into him, by waiting until everyone left to shoot before coming over.

She'd figured Jensen was out filming with the rest of the people. "I'm not mad at you. I just don't like you."

Once again she pushed the plate toward him. "I don't have to like you, do I? It's allowed for someone to not like the great and wonderful Jensen Ford."

"Nope." He took the cupcake and walked back to the lounger. "Everyone by law has to love me." In one hand he held the cupcake and with the other he loosened and dropped the towel.

"Oh my God!" Cassie rushed out of the backyard toward the white house next door.

Jensen's laughter followed her. "Have a nice day, Cupcake Cassie."

"What an ass." Cassie grumbled and then couldn't help but chuckle at his antics. It wasn't that she was a prude, but after a long spell without sex, the last thing she needed was to see a hot and naked Jensen Ford. Not just any actor but the one voted "Sexiest Man Alive" by *People* magazine.

Cassie climbed the two steps to the side doors and entered

her friend Tesha's house, from where they catered.

"Hey there," Tesha Washington, looked up from the table where she sat drinking what looked to be sweet tea. "What's the frown about?"

"That damn Jensen Ford. He's so annoying." Cassie pulled back a chair and sat. "I think he enjoys tormenting me."

Her friend was shorter than her by about three inches, and cute as a button. With a pixie hair cut, caramel skin and expressive brown eyes that met hers at the moment with an amuse smirk.

"Cassie, Jensen picks because you react. He's actually a nice guy if you give him a chance. But he loves to mess around."

"He's laying over there, naked as a jay bird, caught me unprepared." She plopped down and placed her elbow on the table to rest her chin in her hand. "Besides, you're biased because you're engaged to his brother. Jensen has to be nice to you. And he's kind of scared of you."

"He is, isn't he? He shouldn't outside naked. We'll have a swarm of screaming fans attack." Tesha chuckled.

"Uh huh. The man seemed unconcerned. He's sitting over there now eating a cupcake and probably getting crumbs in places I don't want to think about." Cassie shook her head when Tesha laughed. With a sigh, Cassie reluctantly shuffled to get her purse. "I better head to the shop."

"I'll go with you to town." Tesha stood and went toward her bedroom. "Let me just grab my bag. I don't want to be home when the movie crew finishes up and decides to hang around. They expect the kitchen to be open twenty-four hours."

S‍WEET I‍NDULGENCE WAS nestled between a boutique and a gift shop. The store had a welcoming pink and brown awning to match the lettering on the cupcake shop's door, which was done in large curly letters.

Cassie eyed the ingredient-laden shelves, mentally assessing which ingredients she had on hand. Normally each day she sold six types of cupcakes, changing them daily. The only constant was her best-selling Ooey-Gooey Caramel.

"Chocolate Dream, Warm Sugar Vanilla, Banana Crème Pie, Red Velvet and Strawberry Cream," she called over at Tesha, who sat at a table a marker in hand prepared to write on a sign that would be placed outside the door.

Tesha had the most beautiful handwriting, and whenever she came to the shop, Cassie would get her to write the flavors of the day on her dry erase sign.

"Are you making all those today?" Tesha wide eyes met hers. "It's almost noon."

Cassie sighed. "I suppose you're right, I didn't realize most of the morning was gone. I'm usually done at your house by ten and here no later than ten thirty." She eyed the case. "Looks like Carol made three flavors," she said referring to one of the town's widows who helped her part-time when she wasn't cooking at Tesha's. "The banana, chocolate and vanilla are done. I suppose I'll just make two others. It will be a five-flavor day. Scratch the Red Velvet."

Once she began mixing ingredients, she became lost in the process. Tesha found a top forty station on her old radio and began to pull canisters and measuring tools to cook right beside her. Cassie could not have asked for a better friend. When she'd moved to Lovely, Tennessee, it was to nurse not just her ailing grandmother, but her broken heart as well. Never expected to meet someone like Tesha, who quickly became her confidant and best friend.

It was a shame that so soon after meeting, Tesha became engaged to Adam Ford, and now planned to move to Nashville once they got married. Although it was not so far, they would not have these times anymore. Days that revolved around catering for the movie crew in the mornings and making cupcakes at Sweet Indulgence through the afternoons.

"How is Adam?" Cassie placed her bowl under the mixer and turned the knob. "When will he be in town?"

Tesha's face brightened. "He's been here twice already this week. Drove up after work. But I told him to stay in town until the weekend. I don't like him driving back and forth so much. He has to get up at five to get to work on time."

"I'm sure he doesn't consider it too much of a sacrifice to spend time with you. I think it's romantic that he has a hard time staying away." Cassie looked up when the bell over the door jingled and two teenage girls walked in.

The girls both ordered a banana cupcake and coffee and sat down, immediately engrossed with their cell phones.

Several cars passed the shop. Soon downtown Lovely would be bustling with shoppers either heading to Miller's Hardware across the way, the boutique next door, or her shop. A teenage boy looked through the window at the girls and they began to whisper in rushed tones, their eyes darting toward the door.

Kayce, her brother was about their age. Cassie hadn't seen him in months but talked to him regularly on the phone. He remained in Nashville, living with their mother and her latest husband. As soon as he graduated, Cassie made him promise to enroll in a community college not too far from Lovely.

Once her mother stopped getting child support for him, Cassie had no doubt, she'd not fight her on it. Not that her mother was necessarily a bad one, just spent more time trying to keep a man than parenting.

A short while later, with the display case filled, and she was ready for the mid-day shoppers.

It was late in the afternoon that Cassie and Tesha were able to sit down and drink a cup of tea, relaxing in the lull.

"My car is dying. I'm so grateful for the movie. The extra money from catering will help me buy another car. I think the Kia is beyond repair. It barely cranks anymore."

Tesha shook her head. "It's hard to keep cars for long, they don't last more than six or seven years, it seems." She took another sip and studied the Kia through the window. "You're welcome to use my truck whenever you have deliveries that are out of town. It's not much newer than yours, but it runs great. Plus, it will give me an excuse to drive Jensen's Jag."

"Or maybe I can borrow the Jaguar." Cassie laughed. "I can see his expression if I slap a magnetic 'Sweet Indulgence' sign on his classic super-expensive baby and pack it full of cupcakes."

Her friend let out a loud peal of laughter. "Can you imagine if I transport market produce in it?"

"He would die."

Chapter Two

"This is a comfortable bed, don't you think?" Vanessa Morgan spoke matter-of-factly. Her hands splayed on his hips, the actress held him in place atop her. Her eyes flickered past Jensen to the camera crew. "I will have to ask what type of linens they are." She shifted and reached under the pillow for her cell phone. "Damn it, I'm missing a great party. While we shoot here in Hicksville, my friends are having a marvelous time back in LA."

"You'll live." Jensen yawned, ready to get the scene over with. He studied the dark red silky sheets. "Maybe they'll give them to you." Unable to help it, Jensen pulled a corner up and covered his bare butt.

"Don't cover us up. It's too damn hot, I don't want to sweat and have to get my makeup redone," Vanessa whined.

Jensen looked over his shoulder to gauge where the cameras were. It never stopped being awkward. Naked as the day he was born in front of twenty people while they adjusted camera angles and lighting to best show off all the skin. Not that he was shy by any stretch, but under the lights, every pimple, hair, and defect was on display.

He gritted his teeth. "Would you mind not moving so much?"

Her eyes snapped to his face. "Oooh…why, Jensen Ford,

are you getting a bit excited?" Vanessa's lips curved into a feline-like smile. "It would prove interesting. Make the scene more realistic if we get into it."

"No, it would not." Jensen closed his eyes and thought of puke, then followed it by visualizing a toilet full of poop. That Vanessa's breasts were pressed against him or that she only wore a tiny thong did not help. Neither did the attractiveness of the actress who lay beneath him. She was beautiful, with waist-length silky sable brown hair and a perfect body from hours of exercise and very little eating.

"Maybe we should redo this scene again. Alone." She slid her hand down his back and cupped his ass. "I'm game if you are."

That was the problem. Vanessa was always game. Unlike his brother, Adam, who'd slept with her years ago, right after returning from the war, Jensen had managed to keep from sampling her generous offers. Not that he wasn't attracted, but the timing was off. Currently he was dating Selene Bales, Hollywood's current A-list baby. And no matter what the tabloids spewed, he was a one-woman man.

Vanessa adjusted under him, and he closed his eyes and envisioned a cupcake…then for some reason, Cassie Tucker's image came front and center.

He grunted. Yep, wrong image.

"Oh. What is that?" Vanessa winked up at him. "Happy to be on top of me all of a sudden?"

"Don't move." He groaned and looked over his shoulder as someone pulled the covering off his butt. "How much longer?"

"Wanna hook up later?" Vanessa slid her hand down his back until one of her fingers ventured into the top of his butt crack.

"Stop it, Vanessa."

With a soft chuckle, she moved her hand and placed it on his shoulder as directed. "It could be fun."

"I don't know," Jensen replied honestly. "I'll think about it."

"Deep kiss," The director instructed. "Action!"

THE HOUSE WAS bustling with activity when Jensen returned to his brother's home and base of operations for the movie crew. All he wanted was quiet, a place to dig in and hide for a few hours. He walked straight from the front door, past the large living area and kitchen, to the master bedroom. After a few pushups and crunches, he'd shower and crash for the night. He was too exhausted to even think about eating, much less to take Vanessa up on her offer.

The bedroom's lights were on and there was shuffling in the closet. Jensen went to the closet door and looked in. His older brother Adam was digging around in a box and didn't bother to look to see who watched. "I can't find my damn football jersey."

"Why don't you just go buy a new one?" Jensen peeled his shirt off and threw it on to pile of dirty clothes on the closet floor, right next to where Adam stood.

The glare Adam gave him made him take a step back. "Because it's my lucky shirt." He slid a look to the pile of dirty clothes. "I'll be glad when all this is done, and I can have my house back."

Jensen lowered and began doing pushups. "Why? It's not like you're moving back in. When you're in town, you stay at Tesha's."

"This house is not a place for strangers to take over. It's my home," Adam grunted, and tore open another box. "Where the hell is it?"

"What do you plan to do with the house, anyway?" Jensen's arms were tiring, but he pushed on.

His brother didn't stop tunneling through the items the box. "Probably keep it. I don't know, rent it out or something. I haven't decided. It belonged to my buddy, and I hate to sell it."

Vincent Bailey and Adam served together in Afghanistan. His brother's friend died as a result of sniper fire, even after Adam had dragged him to his helicopter and flown him to the closest medical unit. He'd left Adam the old Victorian and a car, which Adam also restored and drove on occasion.

When Jensen's arms threatened to give out, he flipped to his stomach and began to do crunches. "I kinda like this house too."

He frowned up at Adam who'd stood over him with a shirt over his shoulder. "Found it. Joined the city football league in Nashville. Playing tomorrow against the Lebanon Hornets."

"Hornets? What's your team's name?"

Adam toed the edge of the rug. "Trailblazers." He shrugged. "Gotta go. Tesha and I are driving back to Nashville today. Dinner at the parents' tomorrow, you coming?"

"I sorta got a thing planned with Vanessa."

His brother's raised eyebrows brought back the memory that Adam and Vanessa had hooked up. Immediately any desire to even think about going out with the actress waned. "You know what, yeah, I'll be at the folks' tomorrow."

The first thing Jensen did after showering was to text Vanessa to call off getting together. First of all, he couldn't cheat on Selene and secondly…yuck, she'd slept with Adam.

An hour passed and he lay in bed, looking at the ceiling. The wind blew hard against the windows and the rumble of thunder was followed by rain. Too restless to go to sleep, he trudged to the kitchen for a snack. It was almost ten now and most of the crew was tucked in their rooms.

Chad Simpson, a cameraman, sat on the couch watching television. He looked up when Jensen entered and raised a hand in greeting.

There were leftover makings for a sandwich in the fridge. Jensen grabbed some sliced beef, cheese, a cupcake, and a bottle of water. Meal in hand, he plopped down on a chair in the living room and looked to the screen. It was an old war movie.

The cupcake was caramel, his favorite. Cassie usually brought one or two of them when she delivered them in the afternoons. He'd not seen her in a couple days. His lips curved at her reaction to his nudity. For some reason it was fun to pick on her.

Something about Cassie Tucker gripped his attention. She was a combination of sass and innocence. The woman was so different from the many that he'd grown accustomed to in Los Angeles. One minute she got in his face about something and the next, she was blushing and covering her face. Whoever her boyfriend was had to be on his toes all the time to keep up with her. Of course she had a man, a woman that pretty had to have some guy in her life.

The thought of her with someone made him stare at the cupcake.

Who did Cassie date? She seemed to keep busy. Between catering breakfast and her cupcake shop, it left little time for a personal life. If anyone knew about the effect of long hours on a relationship, it was Jensen. Hell, the only reason things worked out with Selene was that they were both actors and understood the business. One had to be a committed to make things work when separated by long hours and distances. Not to mention, in their case, having to cope with the constant allegations of cheating on each other by the tabloids and gossip shows on television.

He considered calling Selene. She was in Australia at the moment. The text she'd sent him last was short and to the point. A quick "thinking of you". They'd never gotten to the "I love you, stage" which suited Jensen fine, since he wasn't sure he loved her. She was totally hot, and they had great chemistry in bed, but at times he wondered when his feelings would develop for her. Caring was more what he felt for her. Even after this separation of almost a month, he didn't miss her. Not really.

A snore caught his attention. Chad's head was thrown back, his mouth wide open. Perfect. Jensen took icing off the cupcake and dropped a huge dollop into the cameraman's mouth.

The guy made a choking sound and began coughing. When he caught his breath Jensen was almost to his bedroom door.

"Son of a bitch!"

Chapter Three

SLEEPLESS NIGHTS WERE the worst. Too tired to sleep and not able to relax, Cassie stretched on her couch and heaved a sigh. The wine she had earlier did little to help. Good thing she didn't have to work the next morning. Once sleep came, it would be nice to sleep in for a change.

A familiar face on the television got her attention. Jensen Ford, front and center on the flat screen. It was an angry scene, he was yelling, the tendons on his neck taut. He wore a torn bloody t-shirt that left little to the imagination. Even with bruising on his face, he was gorgeous.

Cassie sat straight up when the scene switched to him storming into a house where a woman ran to him. The actress began to kiss him and tear his clothes off. When he responded by grabbing her and slamming her against the wall, Cassie's eyes popped wide. "Holy shit," she whispered when the woman wrapped her legs around his hips and began to moan.

With a shaky hand she reached for her remote. Time to turn the television off. The camera moved to show his face, and she stared at the screen, fascinated.

TWO ADDITIONAL GLASSES of wine later, the credits rolled, and Cassie finally pushed the little red button sending her living room into darkness. "Christ, that was hot," she mumbled and headed to her cold empty bed.

Ding. Ding.

Ding. Ding.

"Yeah." Cassie croaked more than spoke into her cell phone. It felt like a brick was imbedded into her forehead. She winced when opening her eyes to the brightness of the room.

She sat up and tilted her head from side to side in an attempt to get the crick out of her neck. "Kayce?"

Her brother cleared his throat. "Are you sick? You don't sound too good."

"I'm just cranky. Didn't get much sleep last night." She eyed the time display on her cell phone. It was ten-thirty, the latest she'd slept in a long time. Perhaps her erotic dreams had something to do with it.

She slapped her forehead, immediately regretting it. But she did not need to revisit her dreams while her little brother was on the phone. "What's up, kiddo?"

"Just wanted to tell you not to come next week. I'm not doing the graduation thing."

Now she was wide awake. Cassie jumped to her feet and shuffled to the kitchen. Tea, very strong tea was in order.

"What the hell are you talking about, Kayce? Of course you're attending. It's a special day."

Her brother was silent. All she could hear was his breathing. Knowing he usually thought before speaking, a quality she didn't possess, Cassie waited.

Finally he spoke, his words quiet and measured.

"I don't have a cap and gown. We didn't make it in time to get it ordered. I can't go through the ceremony without them."

"Shit." Normally she would have apologized for the expletive, but in this case she felt it was warranted. "I'll be there this afternoon. I'll get everything fixed." She hit the numbers on the microwave much harder than necessary after setting the cup of water into the opening. "And don't you worry about a thing. Not only will you walk across the stage, but also you will also have a celebration dinner after."

"I think it's too late. I graduate next week." Despite the words, there was a hopeful lift in Kayce's tone.

"Nope, it's not. I'll speak to the principal and get you a cap and gown. Invite your friends to Bill's Pizza Place. My treat, right after the ceremony."

"Cool." He hesitated. "Mom and Charley are out of town. I told her I wasn't going to do the graduation thing, so they went on a bike ride to Myrtle Beach."

"I'm sorry, honey." She hoped her anger at their mother didn't come across. Kayce was her half-brother, the product of one of her mother's affairs on her father. The one that ended their marriage. Cassie loved Kayce almost like a son, especially since she'd cared for him her entire life. At twelve, when he was born, her mother had a built-in sitter. But since she'd moved out almost six years ago, it had been mostly phone calls.

"No big deal," Kayce interrupted her thoughts. "She'd probably do something to embarrass me anyway. You know how Mama likes to holler and get attention."

Oh yes, she was well aware of her mother's overreaction to things. It never failed; she'd do something to be the center of attention.

Her mother had acted much the same way for weeks after Cassie had found her fiancé in bed with another woman. She'd screamed and cried in front of everyone who came to ask about Cassie.

After handing up with Kayce, thoughts of her failed engagement and how her mother handled things brought the headache back into focus.

The entire fiasco had left her shocked and lost. Not sure what to do next, her grandmother's suggestion to move in with her was exactly what she needed. Moving to Lovely to be with her grandmother and opening the cupcake shop had been the perfect salve to her deep wounds.

When her grandmother met up with girlfriends in a quaint retirement village near Pensacola, Florida, she'd moved there a year later. Living alone in Lovely suited Cassie just fine. She had a good quiet life there.

Cassie's dating life was pretty dismal. Other than a couple of dates over the span of two years, she'd pretty much dedicated her time to her work. It wasn't that she didn't trust men; not all men were the same. It was just hard to move on after such a devastating blow. It was supposed to have been the happiest day of her life. The courtship and engagement had gone by without a hitch. During the wedding plans, she'd noticed Nick had distanced himself and seemed to be on edge, but she'd chalked it up to jitters.

It all became crystal clear in the most cliché event of her life; she'd caught him, pants down and fully locked and loaded between the legs of one of her closest friends.

He'd never told her why he'd done it, never explained his actions, other than to admit it was the stupidest thing he'd ever done. Cassie surmised they'd gotten to know each other during the wedding preparations and one thing led to another.

Instead of staying home to clean her house as planned, she'd go to Tesha's and borrow her truck to go to Nashville. The last thing she needed was hers to break down on the one day she really had to get somewhere. There was no way Kayce would miss his graduation and not have a celebration. He was a good student, not straight A's, but passed all of his classes with a high enough average to not have a problem getting into the community college.

She'd already convinced her mother it was best for him to come stay with her until he began classes in the fall, since the small college was closer to Lovely. Of course once she reminded dear mom about the loss of Kayce's child support, she didn't put up much of a fight. The woman was as shallow as ever.

NOT SEEING TESHA'S truck, she went inside the house. Of course Tesha was gone, Cassie had forgotten Tesha had gone to Nashville for the weekend and probably wouldn't return until later. On Mondays, Debbie and Carol, two women from town, covered the catering job for her and Tesha.

The older women looked up just as Cassie walked in to get a drink of iced tea. "Did Tesha say what time she'd be back today?"

"Sometime this evening," Debbie, a woman with brilliant blue eyes, replied.

"I have to go to Nashville today," Cassie told them dejected. The chair scraped along the wooden floor as she sank into it. "I guess I'll take a chance my clunker will make it."

"You can take my car." A deep voice made her jump.

Jensen peered down at her from the doorway to Tesha's office. "I'm not using it. I have my bike."

"Y—your Jaguar?" She squeaked. "I can't drive that."

"Why not?" His eyebrows lifted, his handsome face serious. "Can't drive a stick?"

"I can drive a stick. It's just that, it's so expensive. No, I can't take a chance that it will get dented or something." Cassie stood and took her keys out of her bag. "Thank you for offering, though."

He followed her outside and took her arm turning her around. "What if you break down? There are spots without a gas station, houses, or a cell phone signal for miles."

Of course he was right, but it made her so nervous that her legs began to shake. It was probably his proximity that caused it along with his offer. "Why are you being so nice to me?" Cassie narrowed her eyes.

"Why are you being so stubborn?" he replied. "How long are you going to be gone?"

"I plan to drive there, see someone at my brother's school and come back. I may have to get a cap and gown, too, so two stops at the most." She looked toward the side of the house where she knew the black Jaguar was parked. "Thank you, but I couldn't possibly accept."

"Fine, I'll drive you, then." He pulled her down the steps, guiding her towards his car.

Cassie pulled her elbow from his grasp. "What about your movie? Won't they be mad if you leave?"

Unfazed by her jerky moves, Jensen took her arm again. "I'm the star of the movie. If I decide to take a day off, they'll shoot around me, and I'll make up the scenes I owe them tomorrow."

Scant minutes later, mouth open, she sunk into the buttery leather and allowed Jensen to buckle her in. Once he slid into the other seat, she finally was able to form a coherent thought. She was driving down a country road alone in a two-seater with Jensen Ford. It was not only unbelievable, but also totally awkward.

He turned to her, his pretty eyes hidden behind dark aviators. "Where are we going?"

"Lebanon."

"Awesome. I know the place well. My parents live there."

"Oh?"

"Yep, actually, do you mind if we stop for dinner?"

Did he just ask her to dinner? Probably at a local restaurant... She wasn't sure what she said in response, because it came out more like a squawk than a word.

"Cool." Jensen must have taken whatever it was for agreement.

Chapter Four

THE PRINCIPAL'S OFFICE sent Jensen straight back to High School. The smells of the cafeteria food in the air, along with the sounds of lockers banging closed, followed by the bell made him glance through the glass door toward the hallway where dozens of students scurried to whichever class was next.

"Just so we are on the same page, Mrs. Clapper? My brother will not only be walking across the stage, but he will be receiving a diploma, right?" Cassie repeated to the middle-aged woman.

The principal of the small high school kept staring at him with ill-hidden admiration. "Yes. Yes, of course. If there's anything else I can do, please do not hesitate to call me."

The woman barely looked to Cassie, speaking to him instead. "The cap and gown will be here in the morning. Have Kayce stop by and pick it up."

"Thank you," Jensen stepped forward and shook the woman's hand. The lady inhaled sharply and leaned forward as if to kiss him.

Cassie stepped in and grabbed his arm. "We'll be on our way. Come on, Waldo."

The principal smiled brightly. "You really should think about filling in for Jensen Ford. You could be his twin, Mr. Dudley."

They made their way to the parking lot and Jensen rounded the car to open the door for Cassie. "Waldo Dudley? Couldn't you think of a better name?"

"Nope." She assumed an innocent expression. "That name suits you perfectly."

It was a nice afternoon and much too early to show up at his parents for dinner. No doubt they'd begin to pepper him and Cassie with questions and his brothers would do something to embarrass him. So he'd prolong their arrival as much as possible. He pushed a button on his cell phone and spoke to a friend while Cassie texted on hers.

The plan of action in place to ensure they arrived just in time to eat was in motion. Why he'd invited her, he wasn't sure. It made sense, since he'd promised to be there for dinner, and she and Tesha, who'd also be there, were close.

It would be the first time since high school that he'd be bringing a woman home. Not that he was bringing Cassie home as a date, but still, his family would automatically jump into either interrogation or matchmaking mode.

His cell phone rang, and he looked at the display. Selene. Of course she'd call now. He'd been trying to contact her for two days. Women must have some sort of competition radar. A bell rang in their heads when their significant others were anywhere in the vicinity of a good-looking woman. Out of the corner of his eye, he glanced at Cassie. Her long auburn waves wrapped around from the wind, and she had her head leaned back on the headrest, eyes closed. *So beautiful.*

So didn't need to go there at the moment. "Hello?" He answered the phone keeping his voice flat. "What's up, buttercup?"

Selene's throaty voice came across clearly. "I'm sorry I didn't return your calls earlier. It's been crazy the last couple days. Long, boring, tiring hours. I have been going straight to bed as soon as I can…"

Cassie opened her eyes and glanced toward him, her whiskey-colored eyes meeting his for a moment before she slid her gaze to the radio. He nodded and she began fiddling with the knobs. The front of her blouse gapped, and he caught a glimpse of the top of her supple breasts.

"Jensen? Did you hear what I said?" Selene sounded aggravated.

"Something about an extension?" He guessed.

"Yes. I may have to stay here another month longer… So I'll miss your brother's wedding."

"I can come there once my shoot is up. I have another three weeks or so." He was about to ask her the exact date her job ended, but she interrupted.

"No. Don't do that. I am not sure of a date yet and besides with this schedule, you'd be bored spending all those hours alone." He heard a man's voice in the background. "I gotta scoot. Smooches." She ended the call before he could reply.

"Where are we going?" Once again Cassie had her eyes closed, her face turned away from him.

He studied the long lines of her elegant neck. "It's a surprise."

Although her moves were still graceful, she turned toward him with a frown. Cassie swallowed and her eyes widened. "I don't like surprises. As a matter of fact, I hate them."

"Oookay, I get that. I'm taking you to one of my friend's businesses. I think you'll like him."

By her drawn eyebrows and lowered gaze, he could see her mulling it over. "I am not in the mood to be fixed up. You are definitely not the person I'd want to do that for me anyway."

"So you aren't in a relationship right now?" His pulse quickened while waiting for her reply.

Cassie let out an aggravated sigh. "Nope. By choice. So call your friend and tell him we're not coming. I am not interested."

He chuckled only because he knew it would annoy her. "I am not hooking you up. I meant you'll like what he does." Jensen wasn't in the mood to fix her up with a guy, either. He reached for the radio and turned the music up. What the hell was he thinking, driving Cassie around town and planning to surprise her?

She was someone he could never aspire to have a relationship with.

The beautiful woman was rare. Cassie Tucker was wholesome and caring. Someone who remained unspoiled regardless of a less than perfect life. Tesha had filled him in on everything about Cassie. His pretty, soon to be sister-in-law seemed to think they'd be a good couple. Cassie was diligent about her younger brother and compassionate enough to uproot her life to care for her grandmother. Not only that, but she was someone who could be lethal to him. A woman like her could bring him to his knees. She had the power to drive him, to look in the mirror and see the ugly truth of what his life had become.

Yes, it would probably not be a problem to get her into his bed. Most women would sleep with him without any effort on his part. His persona, being Jensen Ford, did all the work for him. A notch on the bedpost for sleeping with the current toast of Hollywood was enough to make it impossible to find a challenge.

Sure, at times, Cassie seemed to not care for him, actually seemed to dislike him tremendously, but Jensen had no doubt that if he wanted to sleep with her, Cassie, like most women, would not put up much of a fight.

For an inexplicable reason, the realization made him angry. The emotion simmered just below the surface. What the hell was he doing bringing her to his friend's place anyway. It was the beginning of a familiar cycle. Just setting himself up for the inevitable let down.

"What the heck is wrong with you?" Cassie brought him back to the present. "Slow down."

He eyed the speedometer; the needle hovered at almost eighty. Not good, since the sign he whizzed past read forty-five. He slowed and turned on the next street. Two blocks later, he parked across the street from Delectable Bites.

"This is it. My buddy Tommy owns it." He watched her reaction. First, confusion registered, followed by interest, and then, lastly, a slow smile curved her enticing lips.

"You're friends with Tommy Burgess? He is an amazing baker. This shop has been on the Food Channel numerous times. I came here a couple months ago, but didn't meet the owner."

Jensen exited the car and rounded it to open her door. When her long toned leg stretched out, he lost his train of thought and had to drag his eyes away. This was a bad idea. He should have driven her straight right back to Lovely.

Just a few minutes and he'd take her to his parents. Then

he'd find something to do in a different room. She and Tesha would be preoccupied, and he could avoid her until it was time to drive her home. In the dark. To her empty house.

"Jensen? Are you all right?" Cassie studied him, her brows creased. "You sure are acting strange today." She gave him a curious look. "Stranger than usual, I mean."

He huffed and pretended indifference only to once again lose concentration at the sway of her hips when she crossed the street in front of him. She was about five foot seven inches of enticement, with curves in the right places. It was obvious Cassie did not diet or work out to the point of obsession. This woman was all natural, which made his mouth water at the possibility of seeing all those delicious curves on display.

When she turned to look at him over her shoulder, the wind blew her hair over her face, and she pushed it back. "Come on."

Jensen practically fell off the sidewalk. He took a deep breath and rolled his eyes. "Not like the cupcakes are going to run away. Big deal, they are stupid little cakes with frosting."

She tried to mask the hurt, and how he wished to take the words back. But it was best she knew him for what he truly was: a pompous egomaniac who didn't give a shit about anything but himself and his career. "Let's get inside. I don't want anyone to see me."

The door slammed in his face just as he was about to go in. Jensen jumped back to avoid getting hit in the nose and cursed. He pushed the door open and stepped inside. "Damn it, woman, you could have broken my nose."

Cassie was already at the counter talking to a couple women behind it. Although there were only a couple of patrons,

Jensen ducked his head and pulled his baseball cap down to cover his features as much as possible. The door to the kitchen was to the side of the counter; seeing that the women were engrossed in whatever they spoke about, he slipped through it.

Tommy Burgess never just said hello; he encased Jensen in a rib cracking bear hug. When Jensen was finally able to dislodge himself, he couldn't help but grin at the huge man who beamed down at him. "Long time no see PB!" His friend rarely spoke in low tones. "I've been keepin' up with ya. Can't believe you're dating Selene. She is totally hot." Tommy punched him in the shoulder and Jensen stumbled to the side.

"Nice to see you too, Moose." They grinned at each other like fools. He and Tommy had played football together in High School and were inseparable all four years. They hung out together, studied at each other's houses, and even went to the same college after graduating. Jensen began calling Tommy Moose after his friend christened him with the nickname PB, for Pretty Boy, which annoyed the crap out of him at first.

"What ya doing in town? We need to hang out and grab a beer or something." Tommy looked to the large kitchen where a couple of older women decorated cupcakes. "Hey ladies, I'm gonna leave early today! My friend here is going to buy me a beer!"

The women shook their heads and smiled at them. One Jensen recognized as Tommy's mother came over and hugged him. "Are you eating enough? You're a bit on the skinny side, sweetie." The woman who'd always been like a second mother to him gave him a disapproving once over. She placed her hands on her ample hips. "Come over for dinner more often.

I'll fatten you up."

"Hey, Mrs. Burgess. I have to stay lean. The cameras add some weight."

"Not enough. I've seen your movies." She shook her head and went back to work.

Tommy and Jensen exited the kitchen. He found Cassie sitting at a table with three cupcakes in front of her and a fork in hand. She looked out the window, her lips pursed, as she tasted one of the confections.

When his friend stopped in his tracks, Jensen looked to him. "What?"

"Holy shit! That is one gorgeous creature." Tommy managed to lower his voice for the second sentence. "Is she yours? You bring her from Hollywood?"

"She's just a friend. Well, not really a friend, more like an acquaintance. She needed a ride here to Tucker High."

"Our old stomping ground." Moose laughed at their inside joke. Tucker was their rival in football.

"Yep. Went inside too. Started to spit on the floor." Jensen grinned, only to assume a neutral expression when Cassie stood and looked to them.

Tommy shoved him aside and made a beeline for her. "Hey, there. I'm Tom Burgess, the owner." He looked to the cupcakes on the table. "I see you're doing a taste-testing. What do you think?"

"I don't know how you get so much flavor into your batter. I'm impressed. They are great." She beamed up at Tommy and Jensen almost growled.

His friend took her by the elbow and swept her towards the kitchen. "Let me show you where the magic happens."

They ignored Jensen and disappeared into the back of the shop. With nothing to do, he sat down into her abandoned chair and picked up the fork. He eyed the cupcakes and decided on a chocolate one.

After about half an hour, Tommy and Cassie reappeared. She was wearing a Delectable Bites t-shirt and apron. Her hair was swept up into a long ponytail and she carried a small box, probably filled with cupcakes.

Jensen noticed that Tommy had his arm casually across her shoulders and talking in low tones into her ear. Whatever he said must have been hilarious by the way she threw her head back and laughed.

"We gotta go." He closed the distance and took Cassie's elbow. "Can't be late for dinner."

"Well who knew? I'll see you there," Tommy told him. "I called your Mom and told her you were here, and she invited me."

"That's great," Jensen gritted the words out. What the hell was wrong with him? He had a girlfriend. If Cassie and Tommy hooked up it was no skin off his back. "See you there, Moose."

Cassie laughed at the nickname and met Jensen's gaze. "Let's go, PB."

Jensen glared at Tommy who grinned in return. "Yeah, see you in a bit, PB."

They walked out and he stopped in his tracks. A crowd of women headed straight for the cupcake shop. Word had gotten out. "There he is!" One caught sight of him and screamed. A chorus of shouts erupted. "Jensen! Over here!" Cameras and cell phones were produced. As the women neared, several broke into a run and he gauged the distance to his car. Unfortunately, those wise enough to know it was his, had it surrounded.

"Shit." He muttered under his breath when the first trio reached him. With a cocky grin, he waved at the small crowd. "Hello, ladies. How are ya?"

There was a chorus of shrieks, and everyone began to shout questions to him at once. "What is your next movie? Will you marry me? How can I get a date with you?"

Cassie laughed and shook her head. "How do you deal with it?"

He yanked his cap lower and grabbed Cassie's hand. "I'm used to it. Run."

They managed to make it to the car. He didn't bother to open the door for Cassie but dove into the vehicle and reached across to open the door for her. Unlike him, she took her time getting in while talking to the women.

"We're not an item, just acquaintances. He was nice enough to give me a ride when my car broke down." She lowered the window and waved at one woman who professed to be in love with him and would do anything to marry him. "I'll talk to him," she promised.

When he peeled away careful not to run over the woman who took her time moving from in front of the car, Cassie shook her head. "Poor women. If they knew you better, they wouldn't be so eager to marry you."

"What the heck is that supposed to mean?" Jensen slid a glare at her.

"Nothing." Cassie smiled. "I sure wouldn't want to marry you. You're a pain in the butt."

"That's good news, because I am not attracted to goody-goodies."

She turned in her seat, her mouth slack. "I am not a goody-goody, you don't know anything about me. I can be wild and crazy."

It was hard not to laugh at her attempt to assume an intimidating pose when wearing a cupcake ensemble. He eyeballed her apron. "Yeah, I can see that side of you coming through."

"Oh, hush." She crossed her arms and sat back. "You didn't clarify that we are having dinner at your parent's house. Does your mom like cupcakes?" Bottom lip between her teeth, she looked at the Delectable Bites box on her lap.

Not a goody-goody at all.

"She loves them."

"Oh good, cause I'm already nervous enough and all. I hate to bring something she hates or is allergic to." Cassie fiddled with the hem of her apron. "Do I look alright?"

"You look good enough to eat." He wagged his eyebrows at her.

"Oh, no. Crap. I can't go to your house with all this on! Don't look." She put the cupcakes on the floorboard, tore the apron off and then grabbed the hem of the t-shirt and yanked it up over her head. Wearing only her beige bra, she bent forward and dug the blouse she'd been wearing earlier out of her bag and pulled it on. The pink fabric covered all the bare skin.

"Jensen, watch where you're going," Cassie chastised. "For goodness' sake, I don't want to show up with cupcakes and their dead son."

With gritted teeth, he kept his gaze straight ahead. "You

should warn a guy before taking your clothes off in his car."

Cassie huffed. "It's not like I've got anything you haven't seen. Besides, I'm nothing like those beautiful actresses you do naked scenes with."

She was right about that. Cassie Tucker was nothing like the women he knew. Nothing like them at all.

This woman was much more tempting.

He ran a stop sign and cursed.

"Your driving sucks," Cassie muttered, looking behind them. "You're lucky a police officer didn't see that."

Chapter Five

It was easier for Cassie to concentrate on nitpicking Jensen's driving than to admit she was enjoying the day with him. Although they didn't get along, his thoughtfulness of introducing him to the famous Tommy Burgess who'd risen to stardom on Cupcake Kings, a television show on the Food Channel, had blown her away.

She'd not expected to meet him, had settled for tasting the wonderful cakes on occasion. She'd visited the shop several times, but he'd been away filming the show and was rarely in the shop in person.

Of course, Jensen had breezed right in and not only found Tommy in residence, but seamlessly arranged for her to have a tour of the kitchen. It was turning out to be a stellar day. She'd gotten a cap and gown for Kayce, and then met a celebrity baker, and last but not least, Tommy Burgess had given her a secret recipe for his coconut cupcake which was tucked securely in her purse.

The prospect of meeting Jensen's parents made her stomach tumble. Not because there was anything between them, of course, but just the thought of meeting the famous man's family was enough to unsettle any woman.

She stole a glance at him. Wearing aviators, he leaned back in his seat, his hands on the wheel, in the relaxed posture of a man who was sure of himself. If nothing else, Jensen Ford was very self-assured.

His profile alone made her gaze linger longer than it should. How was it possible for someone to be so breathtakingly attractive?

"How do you stand it?" She blurted out before she could stop herself. "The lack of privacy."

With a cocked brow in her direction, he shrugged his wide shoulders. "The fans are who make me who I am. A lot of actors shun them. I try to not be that way. It's part of life when living the dream. It can be tiring at times, but I remind myself, if not for people watching my movies I wouldn't be making such a good living."

His reply didn't actually surprise her. It was obvious that Jensen loved what he did. A smile curved his sensuous lips. "Sorry about that. I know it's kinda overwhelming for my friends. My brothers hate it. Especially when they get groped. Well, not Caden, he eats it up."

"About your brothers. How do you guys get along? There's four of you, right?"

The look on his face when he turned to her was priceless. He actually beamed. "I've got great brothers. We have a good relationship, all of us. The best thing about them is how they keep me grounded."

He lifted up a hand, one finger up. "Tristan can be a bear. He's the oldest and has that bossy thing going, but he's a great guy. Stepped in and took over my dad's marketing company even though I think he really wanted to go into architecture."

He grinned at her and her heart flipped. Damn his sexiness. "He owns a plane now so that makes him happy, I suppose. The guy is so serious, he can laugh without smiling." Jensen chuckled at his own joke.

"What about Caden? He's the youngest, right?" Cassie had caught sight of all the brothers on occasion, but Caden was the one who hung out with Jensen more often.

"Yeah, that's my little bro. He's not right in the head. Almost thirty and moved back in with my parents. Caden is crazy. Loves women but hates to be away from home for long. I think he has separation anxiety, which is crazy since he's a homicide detective and all that."

Cassie laughed. "You make him sound like a walking contradiction. Maybe he just needs some time at home to get his bearings after seeing the things he does when on the job."

Brows lifted, he let out a whistle. "You might be right. I'd not have thought of that. Then there's Adam. You know him." He left the sentence hanging. Neither needed to expand on Adam, who seemed to be recovering from severe PTSD.

"What about you?" She faced him. "Which brother are you?"

His face hardened for a moment and his brows furrowed. Cassie waited for some sort of wisecrack. Instead he surprised her. "The one who wishes he was home more cause he misses out on all the important stuff. That guy that no one outside the family really knows."

"So have I seen the real you?"

His right shoulder lifted and lowered with nonchalance, although the twitch in his jaw said otherwise.

"You've seen all the glory that is Jensen Ford." So he was back to being the jackass.

"And I'm in awe," Cassie replied dryly. She'd seen two

sides of him; maybe in the midst of it was the real Jensen. It would be interesting to see how he acted at home.

They continued on in companionable silence until Cassie's cell phone rang. She answered without looking at the display.

The voice on the other end took her by complete surprise. Nick's familiar drawl greeted her. "Hey, Cassie. I'm surprised you answered. How are you?"

She slid a look towards Jensen, who didn't seem to be listening in, and wished she wasn't in the car with him at that moment. She'd not heard from her ex-fiancé in a year and now all of times he decided to freakin' call. "I'm good. What's going on?"

"I can't stop thinking about you. I'm hoping we can meet. I can come there to Lovely. Maybe we can have dinner or something, and, you know, talk."

Seriously? She gritted her teeth, biting words like "fuck off" and "go to hell". Instead she let out a breath. "I can't. Right now is not a good time. I will call you when I can talk." *And able to loudly tell him to go to hell.*

"Oh. Okay." Nick sounded dejected. "I have some news."

Cassie rolled her eyes. Jensen had turned in her direction now and gave her a questioning look. She smiled as if her phone call was a pleasant one. "I'll call you back and you can tell me all about it." She pressed the end button and dropped her phone back into her purse.

"We're here." Jensen drove through an open wrought iron gate down a bricked drive that lead to a beautiful plantation-style home. The house was one story, but it sprawled in both directions. She imagined, it went deep too, to have housed the wealthy family of six.

"Hacienda sweet hacienda," Jensen said once he pulled up, and jumped out of the car. He opened her door, and she accepted his hand to get out. It was the first time, other than shoving him out of her way and him pulling her through the hoard of fans, that they touched in a friendly way. His hand was firm and held her in a tight grip, not strong enough to hurt her, but in a way that communicated it was up to him to let her go first.

Keeping her hand in his, he guided her to the front door, and only when he reached for the knob did he release it. A mixture of surprise that she'd enjoyed his touch and the anxiety at entering the Ford's large home made her take a deep breath to calm down.

They walked into a good-sized entryway. Straight ahead was a tall wall with built-in shelving that housed horse statues and family pictures. To the right and left were massive archways to other rooms. Cassie noticed a sitting room on the right, and to the left opened to what looked like a library. They walked through the left archway, and she gasped at the enormous kitchen and dining room combination.

"We never had a separate dining area. Always eat in here," Jensen explained, once again taking her hand and pulling her through the room to a floor to ceiling windowed wall. French doors opened to a beautiful bricked in patio with loungers under a portico. A long refreshing pool was a few feet away, another set of loungers on one side, and what looked like a bar with chairs on the other. There was a round table and wicker seating on the left side where Tesha and a woman she recognized as Jensen's mother sat. With them was Caden. To the left of the group on a lounger was a teenage girl flipping through a magazine with a bored expression.

Tesha and Jensen's mother got to their feet at the same time. Although his mother gave her a curious look, she addressed Jensen first. "You came. I'm so glad. Adam told me you were going to try to make it." She kissed her son's cheek when he bent to hug her.

With a wide smile, Tesha stood back and waited for the matriarch of the family to speak to Cassie first. Miriam Ford, a striking petite woman, held out her hand and Cassie grasped it.

Her bright blue eyes met hers. "Hello, darling. You're Tesha's friend Cassie, right?"

"Yes, ma'am. Jensen was nice enough to give me a ride to Tucker High School today since my car is horribly unreliable." At the mention of the high school, the teenager dropped her magazine and stared at Cassie with interest.

"It's great you're here," Tesha exclaimed, her smile brighter. "We can spend the afternoon together. We're planning the wedding, and another set of eyes would be helpful."

"Very true." Jensen's mother took Cassie's arm. "We can't seem to concentrate on the subject. Keep veering off down rabbit trails."

Miriam stopped and looked at Jensen. "Honey, go fetch us more lemonade, please. Don't forget to add a splash of bourbon and a mint sprig."

It was astonishing to see the superstar being treated like a normal person, no special treatment from his family. He went to the teenager and ruffled her curly hair. "Hey, shortstop, what you doing?"

The teen glared up at him. "Stop, Uncle Jen. It took me

forever to get it under control."

Uncle? Cassie looked to the girl with curiosity.

Tesha took her arm. "Cassie, this is Nahla. She is Tristan's daughter." The girl had the most amazing caramel-toned skin, which made her pale hazel eyes stand out. She was gorgeous.

Nahla gave her a short wave. "Hi."

It was strange to think of Tristan as a father; the man seemed so closed off all the time. She was dying to ask Tesha about the teen. Once they got back to Lovely, she was going to drill her friend for information.

Before long, she and the other two women were engrossed in bridal magazines and had a laptop between them with more wedding idea pictures.

The French doors opened, and two brothers stepped through: first, Jensen, his good looks making her look twice; then, the youngest brother, Caden. They each held two glasses of lemonade with sprigs of mint.

Cassie looked to Tesha, who smiled widely. Miss Miriam had taught her sons well. They knew how to serve an attractive cocktail.

Caden's long strides brought him closer. His piercing blue eyes pinned her with a curious look. Jensen handed Nahla the one glass with a cherry marking it as non-alcoholic. Then he handed Cassie her drink and smiled. "I'm Caden, I don't believe we've met."

In spite of herself, she blushed at his close scrutiny. Cassie took his proffered hand. "Cassie Tucker. I'm Tesha's friend, from Lovely."

His eyes slid to Jensen. "So you're not Jensen's friend?"

Unsure of what to say, she swallowed and looked at Jensen,

who'd given Mrs. Ford her drink and was watching with a scowl on his face.

"I would describe us more as acquaintances than friends," she finally said, taking a drink of the tasty cold spiked lemonade. "This is delicious, thank you."

Caden favored the other two brothers. With dark chestnut brown hair and blue eyes, he had the same large muscular frame and wide shoulders, but unlike Adam and Tristan, this brother seemed easygoing, with a carelessness about him that could trick someone into thinking he didn't have one single worry.

Cassie studied him, and he must have felt it, because he looked to her and then she saw it. It was brief, but his eyes widened just a bit. He wondered if she could see the shadows that he tried hard to hide.

Yes, she'd seen them. It was the same look she saw in the mirror many times.

Jensen came over and sat down on a chair next to hers. He stretched his long legs and looked at the pile of magazines on the table. "Why don't you just hire someone to do all this? Dad said you've been at it for days."

Cassie joined in the circle of incredulous stares directed at the actor whose wide eyes bounced from one to the other. "What?"

"Jeez, Uncle Jen, you don't know anything." Nahla shook her head. "This is the fun part of a wedding. Picking the colors and the theme. We can't let a planner do that."

"What did you pick?" Jensen smiled at the teenager astonishing Cassie at how comfortable he was around different people. Jensen was born to be well-liked. Except for her. She was still not sure if she liked him. He'd not been nice to her before this day.

Nahla jumped to her feet and held out a torn-out magazine page. "I picked the colors. They are going to be Neapolitan."

"What does that look like?" Jensen took the piece of paper and stared at it. "I don't see any color other than brown, pink and white."

He was kidding the teen, but Nahla didn't notice. She put her fists on her hips. "It's a color theme. Like the ice cream. The colors are chocolate, strawberry and vanilla." She huffed. "Duh."

He looked to Cassie. "Which flavor are you?" His voice as low and Cassie knew he wasn't talking about colors. "I would guess vanilla."

Laughter burst from Caden and Adam, who stood at the door. Adam came over and kissed Tesha, then turned to Jensen. "That was the lamest pickup line ever."

"Like you would know," Jensen threw back with a wide grin. "It was a classic."

Adam shook his head. "I would say it pretty much ranked right above the time Tristan bought a girl a hot dog and said…"

"Boys!" Mrs. Ford interrupted. "Let's ask Cassie what she thought?"

Cassie was sure her face was bright red. Her cheeks on fire she took a gulp of the drink. "I didn't realize it was a line. I think he really did want to know which flavor I liked." She feigned an innocent expression.

Everyone laughed except Nahla, who'd gone back to her lounger, obviously deciding adults were dumb.

Mrs. Ford looked to Adam. "Is Tristan coming for dinner?"

Adam shook his head. "Nope. He has a business thing tonight. He said that he will come by this weekend."

The sons went inside a few moments later and Cassie looked to Tesha, who was cutting out a picture. "What are they up to?"

Her friend gave her a wide-eyed smile. "The best thing about marrying a Ford is that they can cook. Miss Miriam makes the main course, and they make the sides. Salad, vegetable dish, that sort of thing."

Mrs. Ford leaned forward and winked. "They can all cook a special dish too. Adam makes the best lasagna. Caden cooks a great pot roast."

"What's Jensen's?" Cassie asked before she could help it. For one, she really could not imagine him cooking.

Mrs. Ford gave her an assessing look. "He's the best cook of all of them. Makes great tacos and Mexican rice. His meatloaf is great, too. Of all the boys, he's the one that spent more time in the kitchen with me. He loves to cook."

"I didn't know that," Tesha interjected. "I wonder how often he cooks now."

They sipped and continued eating. Cassie noted Mrs. Ford did not bring up Tristan, and she wondered if he was the only one that was exempt from cooking, being the oldest. If she couldn't imagine Jensen cooking, the thought of the morose Tristan donning an apron seemed farfetched.

"What about Tristan?" Tesha didn't seem to have a problem bringing up the oldest brother.

Mrs. Ford's expression brightened. "How could I forget to

mention my oldest. He's our grill master. Fights over it with his dad."

"Anybody home?" a deep voice bellowed and was greeted by the brothers. The cupcake king had arrived.

THE DRIVE BACK to Lovely was like night and day from earlier. Jensen remained silent, his jaw clenched.

Worried more about whether to call Nick back or not took precedence over Cassie wondering what crawled up Jensen's butt. She looked to her cell phone and saw a text from Tesha. She was also returning to Lovely, following behind them.

"Tesha needs to stop and use the bathroom," Cassie told Jensen who gave her a stiff nod.

"I think there's a convenience store just up ahead."

As soon as they pulled into the small country merchant's parking lot, Jensen exited the car and made a phone call.

Tesha came to the car window after using the bathroom. "Sorry about that. I should have gone before leaving."

Cassie looked to Jensen. "Can I ride with you? I'm not sure why I'm in his car. I have to go to your house to get my car, so it doesn't matter who I ride with."

"Sure." Tesha waved at Jensen who stood a short distance away. "I'm taking Cassie away from you."

Jensen gave them a short wave and returned to his call.

Cassie rolled her eyes. "He's in a bad mood."

Once ensconced in Tesha's car she let out a breath. "Thanks, he's acting strange as usual. Not speaking to me."

"I bet he's jealous," Tesha replied with a wide smile. "Caden and Tommy shadowed you the entire time."

"They were just being nice." Cassie frowned. "Besides, Jensen doesn't like me. He is dating that superstar Selene. Figure the odds of him being attracted to a country bumpkin like me."

"You are a bumpkin, aren't you?" Tesha laughed. "But you're a pretty bumpkin."

"Oh, hush." Cassie let out a snort, which sent them into fits of giggles.

Chapter Six

JENSEN WAS RELIEVED that Cassie left with Tesha. He finished his phone call with his agent and let out a frustrated sigh.

The man wanted him and Vanessa to play out a romance between them to help sell the movie. He'd already arranged for them to take an impromptu trip to Cabo, leaving a trail of breadcrumbs for the media. It would delay filming for a couple of weeks, but the publicity team felt it was imperative they fight the rumors of Selene dating her costar and not make him seem less than Alpha male by being dumped. This way it would look like both he and Selene had ended the relationships amicably and moved on.

It struck him that Selene had not mentioned her publicist's media tactic. He understood how the industry worked. Agents were forever pushing a romance between costars to the tabloids. His first reaction was to contact her and let Selene know it was not real so she could tell the tabloids during interviews they were on friendly terms and keep the media guessing.

He expected the same in return.

Since she'd gone to Australia after only a few months of dating to go shoot a movie, so they hadn't had time or thought of discussing what to do when things like perceived dating and other tabloid rumors came up.

He'd met Selene just after his last movie, which had been an international sensation. It had been a whirlwind romance, so fast and crazy, he couldn't remember who'd approached her first and how they'd ended up being exclusive.

Jensen dialed her number as he drove toward Lovely. When she didn't answer, he left a voice mail. It was afternoon in Australia, so she was probably working. He needed to reach her before leaving for Cabo. Once he got to town, he'd send her a text as well.

He wondered if Tesha would get on his case again for not acting like he'd been with Cassie in the car. Adam's fiancée was fiercely protective of her friend.

Admittedly, he had been rude. But every time he opened his mouth to say something, the first thing that came to mind was to ask whether she was interested in Caden. The two had been inseparable the entire evening. Sat next to each other at dinner, discussing some nonsense television show both watched. Laughing at inside jokes no one else got. No sooner than Caden would move away, Tommy took his place. Jensen didn't get a chance to even blink in her direction.

Even his mother had made a comment about how well the two got along. As if Caden deserved a good woman like Cassie. The womanizer would probably use her and move on without a backwards glance.

He hit the steering wheel and let out a grunt. Why should he give a crap? It wasn't as if she couldn't take care of herself. Besides, the woman had more spunk than he'd given her credit for. When she'd taken her shirt off in the car, he'd almost pulled over to watch her get dressed. Her generous breasts were barely held back with the flimsy material of the bra she wore, and all that satiny skin on display made it almost impossible not to stare.

How had he not noticed how sensually appealing she was? He knew she was pretty and something about her called to him from the first day he they'd met. However, now that he'd had a sneak peek at what she hid under her clothes, Jensen wanted more. He wanted to see the long legs on full display, her perfectly round ass free from any type of covering.

"Shit." Jensen pulled his car to the side of the road. Blue lights flashed into his mirror. "Damn that woman."

MARK SMITH WAS the name of someone boring and with no personality. But this agent was anything but. Wearing jeans, a crisp white shirt and a sweater vest, the slender but fit blond man looked more like a model than a Hollywood agent. With pale eyes and a gaunt face, he gave the impression of gentleness. However, those that knew him would consider him more a pit-bull than a poodle. Once he sank his teeth into something, he didn't let go. He'd represented Jensen for five years, and in that time, he'd been the main one responsible for catapulting him to mega stardom.

Right now Mark sat in a lawn chair at Adam's house in Lovely. In the screened-in porch, the crisp air made the early evening a comfortable time of day to be outside. Blending into the casual setting with a tall glass of club soda, Mark's eyes went from Jensen to Vanessa.

"What we need is a lot of PDA. But at the same time act as

if you're hiding from the cameras. You know, look around before kissing, that kind of thing."

Vanessa leaned forward with a pinched brow. "Could you pick a location more original than Cabo? How about England? It's so romantic."

"I think we should stay on this side of the planet," Jensen said, bored with the conversation that had lasted way longer than necessary. They'd already gone over what to wear, locations where they had to be, posing, times and dates.

"If I'm leaving in a couple days to act as if I'm being lovey-dovey with her, I need to talk to Selene and let her know," Jensen said, garnering a pointed look from his manager.

"I'm going to pack." Vanessa stood and kissed Mark on each cheek. "Maybe you and I can go to England sometime." She gave a short giggle and walked away.

"Is she serious?" Mark's eyes followed Vanessa's departing figure. "I'd bang her."

Jensen kept to himself that the actress didn't seem to be too choosy. She'd already slept with some the onsite crew. "She's energetic. You should."

"Have you?" Mark lifted a brow. "Don't want to piss in your puddle."

"I try to stick one woman." Jensen looked at his beer. "So what was that look you gave me when I mentioned calling Selene?"

His agent squirmed and looked away from him. "You know she really is seeing Zack Acker, right?"

It was interesting to note Mark in any kind of discomfort; the man rarely showed emotion of any kind. "Look, Jensen, I like you as a person, and I feel as if I'm also your friend. So I need to tell you that I don't think they're faking it."

His gut knotted. There was a first time for everything, but he didn't expect to be cheated on by the woman who'd made no qualms about wanting him and pushing for a relationship.

"What makes you say that?"

"From what I understand, they are sharing his trailer on site in Australia. He brought her home a couple weeks ago for a family event. They kept it pretty well hidden until someone caught them at the airport going back to Australia." He gave him a penetrating look. "Don't you and her talk?"

Not much in the last couple months. He had to admit, they texted more than talked lately. "Not often enough, it seems."

Long after Mark went back inside, Jensen sat outside. When he popped the cap on his third beer, he glanced up to see Cassie and Tesha. They pushed a cart with a cake atop it. Cassie coached Tesha along. "Steady. Wait. Slow down. There's a bump here."

He leaned back in the chair and shook his head. "Why don't you just carry it?"

Tesha glanced at him. "Because it's heavy and fragile."

"I'll get it." He stood up.

"No!" both women cried out when he took a step toward them.

"We got this," Cassie held her arms out to block the cake. "If something happens to my masterpiece I'll cry."

With an annoyed huff, he sat back down. "Who gives a shit? The damn thing's gonna get cut anyway."

He studied the cake. It was decorated to looked like a stack of purses. They looked real. Impressive that she could do it with cake batter and icing. "Besides, it's gaudy."

Cassie's eyes rounded and her mouth fell open. He looked away, hating himself for uttering the words.

"A man would say that." Tesha touched Cassie's arm. "Come on, let's get it out of the sun and set up over there under the canopy."

The women continued their slow progress away from him. Tesha glared over her shoulder at him when Cassie was turned away and Jensen rolled his eyes.

AN HOUR LATER, he stood at the back patio watching Vanessa oohing and ahhing over the cake. She'd taken dozens of pictures of it and with it. Obviously it was her birthday. The actress was in seventh heaven, excited to be the center of attention.

She pulled Cassie close and hugged her, then handed her cell phone to Tesha. "Take our picture together, please. Make sure the cake is in it." Vanessa smiled widely.

"You're making all my cakes from now on," the actress told Cassie, who remained reserved. "I mean it, Cassie. You are a genius. I already love your cupcakes. This is the most awesome cake ever. You have all my favorite purses on there."

"She is very gifted." Tesha handed Vanessa a small plate with a sliver of cake.

Jensen's cell phone rang, and he went inside to his bedroom to answer it. Selene sounded groggy. "Hey, sorry it took so long to call you back. My hours have been crazy. There was this huge storm. A freak one…"

She continued for a few minutes describing the damage the

storm had caused to the set and such.

"Are you seeing Acker?" Jensen dove right in, not in the mood for games. "If you are, it would have been nice to give me a heads up."

"I—I don't know what to say." Selene's voice became high pitched. "I mean, it sort of just happened."

"You came back to the states with him. You're staying in his trailer. That just sort of happened too?"

Her breathing was audible. "Shit. I'm sorry. My agent made me keep it from you."

"Why? So you could come across like a cheating bitch? Cause that would be such great publicity right? Maybe that will be the headline of my next interview."

"You wouldn't dare!" Selene shouted. "It's not like that. I mean, we wanted to tell you."

We. "Did you really think I wouldn't find out? When the fuck were you planning to tell me?"

"Look, it started out as PR. I mean he is the man of the hour, it made sense."

So that was it. Acker was the 'man of the hour', Selene's M.O. going from who was on top of the pile at the moment.

Out of the corner of his eye he caught sight of someone passing the door. He went to it and slammed it shut. "Look, fine. Do what the hell you want. But don't expect me to sit back and look like a fucking pansy."

His hand trembled with anger when he pressed the end button.

"Damn it!" The cell phone bounced off the bed and onto the floor when he threw it.

Chapter Seven

A TIMER DINGED and Cassie pulled open the oven door while balancing her cell phone between her ear and right shoulder.

Kayce continued talking, his voice cracking between deep and high pitch. She smiled at the sound of her baby brother going through the stage of turning into a man. At seventeen, he was a bit of a late bloomer, but that was fine with her.

"The guys are excited about hanging out after graduation. Andy wants to know if he can bring his mom. And Jerry said his parents are coming, but they're paying for their meals. I also invited Clara, she's coming alone."

Cassie laughed. "Okay, so we have eight total. Yes, that's fine, and I'll pay for it all. This is a celebration for you, Kayce."

"Cool. But I don't think they'll mind paying," Kayce insisted. "Mom left me some money, I can pitch in too."

"Save your money. You'll need it." Cassie's heart melted at the excitement in his voice.

After a few more minutes of listening to his plans for that day, she hung up with her brother and slid the cupcake pan to the counter then retrieved the second one. A glimpse of dark brown hair at the door made her heart skip. "Oh boy," Cassie mumbled and turned to put another two pans into the oven.

Jensen entered and strolled to the counter. He didn't bother to stop until he lifted the hinged counter and walked behind it to where she stood. "Quiet afternoon, huh?"

He picked up a cupcake and sniffed it, his eyes pinned to hers. "Yum."

Heat rose from her neck until her face felt fevered. Damn him and that pretty face. "You're not supposed to be back here." Cassie snatched the cupcake from him. "And you can't sniff cupcakes either."

For a few moments they only stared at each other, neither spoke nor did they move. Cassie wasn't sure who took the first step to kiss.

All she knew was that feeling Jensen's mouth over hers and being up against his hard chest were overwhelmingly wonderful.

The world ceased to exist as he continued his wonderful taking of her lips, while his hands slid down her body to cup her butt. He lifted her onto the counter, and she slid her arms around his neck. At the moment it was all him, the feel, the taste and the hardness of Jensen Ford.

His tongue probed and Cassie parted her lips to allow him access. The heat from the ovens behind him permeated through the skin, but warmth of his touches went deeper, straight to center of her being.

It had to stop, the rational side of her brain screamed for Cassie to listen, but her body overruled common sense when his palm covered her left breast, and his fingers moved to caress her nipple. Instead of moving away, she grabbed his shoulders to bring him closer. The man was an incredible kisser, and his body oh so felt perfect.

In the distance a bell rang, and Cassie considered how

appropriate to hear chimes at the precise moment her legs wrapped around his waist. He lifted back, his eyes half closed. "I think your oven is ringing."

"What?" It took a few seconds before the words made sense. She wasn't sure, but he may have repeated it twice. "Oven?"

By the time she realized she was sitting on the counter and a moment ago had her legs wrapped around a man in plain view from any passerby, Jensen had donned oven mitts and was pulling overly browned cakes from the oven. He placed them both on the counter with smooth moves of someone used to being in the kitchen. When he pulled the second pan, he set it next to the first. "There, they look fine don't you think?"

Cassie stared at him with rounded eyes. "I don't like you. I'm not sure what just happened."

The one shoulder shrug didn't tell her anything, so Cassie grabbed his arm and turned him to face her. "I mean it. I'm not sure what that was all about."

Jensen lifted a brow, his darkened eyes traveled down her body. "Women like bragging rights. You're probably no different."

"What the hell is that supposed to mean?" Cassie slammed her hand down on the counter, which hit the edge of the pan sending hot cupcakes askew, a few landed on the floor. She ignored them and glared at Jensen. "I'm not a groupie."

"You just said you don't know what happened. You don't like me." Jensen's voice was neutral, a blank expression on his face. He looked down at her, and there was a hard, icy edge to his voice. "It happens to me all the time. It's enjoyable sometimes."

Her hands curled into fists. She had to hold back the urge to slap the look of disdain from his face. "You came here, behind the counter, so don't put it all on me."

"I'm not. Just helping you figure out why you threw yourself at someone you claim not to like." He walked around her and straight out the front door.

"What the hell was that?" Cassie uttered out loud and glared at the doorway. Perhaps she shouldn't have said she didn't like him after humping him like a dog in heat.

"Ugh!" She picked up a cupcake and took a big bite only to spit it out when it burned her tongue. Outside a motorcycle rumbled to life and she saw Jensen ride by, his head forward.

The bell over the door jingled and woman with arms full of shopping bags walked in. "It's hot in here."

"You have no idea." Cassie turned to see the oven door was still open.

THE NEXT MORNING at Tesha's house, the smell of sausage, eggs and biscuits drew the eager film crew for an early breakfast. They'd set up two round tables in the large room between the kitchen and living room. The hum of conversations intermingled with the soft jazz Tesha loved to play.

Cassie kept a nervous eye on the French doors every time they opened. Jensen had yet to make an appearance, and she couldn't help but wonder if she should find him and apologize.

He'd not acted offended, but in all fairness she should not have blurted not liking him. He'd been nice enough to drive her to see about Kayce's school and all. Besides, there had been something about him that had bugged her. He had not seemed himself since the morning before.

"One more batch of eggs and we should be done. Those that haven't made it probably are not planning to eat," Tesha told her, forking sausage into a platter. "I heard voices earlier, not sure if they were leaving or just getting in."

A few seconds later, Vanessa Morgan came down the stairs. She stretched like a cat and sniffed the air. "So much for sleeping in, between the smells and the chatter, it was impossible."

She came to the counter and picked up a piece of toast and nibbled at it. "I'm so hungry today," Vanessa announced, to nobody in particular.

At the sound of footfalls Cassie looked to the stairs, where Jensen appeared. From his mussed hair and rumpled clothing, he'd also been sleeping until a few moments earlier.

He'd spent the night there. Not in his room at Adam's house. Her stomach churned and her chest constricted.

Tesha looked to the actor with a critical eye and then turned to Vanessa with a frown before speaking to Jensen. "Breakfast?"

"Nah. I'll grab something at the house." He walked through the room and straight out the French doors. Everyone seemed to ignore the obvious conclusion that the co-stars had slept together.

Cassie handed the spatula to Tesha. "I'll be right back." She trailed after Jensen out the side doors. He was almost to the front porch next door when she caught up with him.

"Hey."

Yawning and scratching his head, he turned to look at her. "Hey."

"I wanted to apologize for what I said yesterday." She let out a breath. "After what you did, taking me to the school and to your parents...I shouldn't have snapped at you."

"Okay." He looked past her. "Anything else?"

He certainly knew how build a wall, she would give him that. At the moment once again she was having a hard time liking him.

"Nope. That was it." She turned on her heel and walked back to Tesha's. Why had she even bothered?

He was definitely an actor, because the man who'd dismissed her just now was not the same one who'd driven her to his hometown and took her to the cupcake shop. Which one had come to the bakery? Why had he come and kissed her senseless?

Cassie brushed a tear away. Her gut churned with jealousy. There was nothing between her and Jensen, of course. But the knowledge he'd slept with another woman hurt, for whatever reason.

WHEN THE FRONT door closed behind him Jensen slacked against it. His chest so tight he fought to breathe. For the first time in a long time real tears stung his eyes. How tired he was of the same thing. Of meaningless sex. Of women wanting to be with him because of who he was. The hurt of being cheated on by Selene led him to make two back-to-back stupid mistakes that would cost him.

He'd gone to see Cassie, to talk, to try to have a normal day. When he'd woken the day before all he could think about was the need to be with someone who understood normality. Although he'd not gone on a date in a long time, the thought of asking Cassie to go with him on a ride in the country had excited him. Planned to first flirt a bit and then ask her out.

When they'd kissed he had been sure she'd agree; things had gone better than he expected is what he'd thought.

Dumb, so damned stupid.

The first words she'd uttered after the best kiss he'd experienced was to tell him she didn't like him. Thank God he was an actor because it had taken all his skills to keep from showing the hurt he felt at the words that cut into him. Straight to the gut, Cassie hadn't held back what she really thought about him.

To complete the campaign of stupidity, he'd come back, drank too much and took Vanessa up on her offer to spend the night with her. Sometime around two or three, they'd stumbled to her room. Too drunk to remember much, he wasn't sure he'd actually done anything, not until the morning when she'd taken care of him before the sun had even risen.

Of course the movie crew expected it to be a stunt to get tongues wagging, as most of them knew Mark's gossip mill plan.

He didn't care about them knowing, but he wasn't too sure how he felt about Tesha. Her disapproving look didn't sit well. But she'd get used to it. If she was to be his sister-in-law, there were a lot more women in his future she'd hear about.

He'd not looked at Cassie, not that it mattered. Since she didn't care for him, she probably didn't give a shit what he did.

Jensen went to the kitchen and opened the refrigerator, allowing the cold air to blast into him. He grabbed a bottle of water and chugged the entire content, washing down three headache pills that were kept handy on the countertop. While he waited for the coffee cup to fill from the automatic maker, he looked through the side windows toward Tesha's house.

Why had Cassie followed him? The last person he was in the mood to talk to this morning was her. There was no way in hell he would allow her near him ever again. What he'd felt the day before was too much like caring. It was clear after her statement that she would not mind sleeping with or making out with Jensen Ford the super-star, but when it came to the man, she didn't like him.

Unlike her, he could see himself with someone like Cassie. She was the type of woman a man married, sunk into her pliant body for years without tiring of her. A woman who could fulfill fantasies and make a guy hurry home. Very dangerous thoughts, he admitted with a grunt, and took his coffee with him as he trudged to the bedroom.

He'd move on.

Continue the make-believe relationship with Vanessa and once the movie was done take some time off. Maybe ride across the country or something. Just him and the bike. No need for anyone else in his life.

Chapter Eight

"Where's the graduate?" Tesha asked Cassie as they sat in the cupcake shop a week later. It was an hour before closing, almost five. Kayce had come to stay with Cassie after his graduation, a couple of days before. He was only staying for a few days and then going to Myrtle Beach for two weeks.

Cassie smiled at her friend, who'd kept the conversation away from Jensen. Hadn't even asked her why she'd gone after him the other morning.

"Kayce's at home. Probably in front of the television. He should be packing, but no doubt will wait until the last minute."

"He's got two days." Tesha shook her head. "It's nice of his friend's parents to take the boys to the beach for a summer break."

"Kayce is so excited about it. Said they get the first floor to themselves, at the beach house."

Tesha laughed. "A small taste of independence. Of course when it comes time to eat and such, they'll want parents nearby."

"Of course," Cassie agreed with a chuckle. "Once he gets back, in three weeks, he starts classes at Newton City College. I only get him to myself for a few days."

"You can see him on weekends." Tesha reassured her. "Plus it will give him a chance to grow up slowly."

"That's true." Cassie sighed. "I was hoping to give him my car when I buy another one, but it's acting up again. So frustrating."

"I have an idea," Tesha told her with a wide grin. "I won't need my truck when I move to Nashville. I'll gift it to Kayce as a graduation present."

"I can't let you do that. We'll pay for it." Cassie stood and refilled their cups with fresh decaf. "You're too generous, but I insist on paying you something for it."

Tesha gave her a droll look. "I don't think it's worth more than a grand. How about that?"

Although she knew Tesha's truck was worth a lot more, she was grateful. It would answer her prayers so that Kayce could get back and forth from school to work with her on the weekends. "All right, I'll give you the money on one of the saddest days ever."

"What?" Tesha licked frosting from her fingers and swallowed her cake. "What do you mean?"

"The day you move. I won't have my bestie close by anymore." Cassie frowned into her coffee.

"What about Eliza?" Tesha asked referring to the friend of Cassie's who worked at the Lovely Diner. "She's very nice."

"True." Cassie had to agree. "But she's always with Deputy Castro. They are inseparable."

"That will get old soon and she'll need a woman friend." Tesha smiled. "At least that's what I hear happens."

She stood to stretch. "I better head home. Adam will be here soon."

"Uh huh." Cassie gave her a teasing look. "I have a hard time thinking being with the man you love ever gets old."

Minutes later Cassie leaned her elbows on the counter and looked through the shop's windows. Everyone went on with their lives. Soon Tesha would be gone, and she'd remain behind, in her shop center of Lovely, with no life. Sometimes it was more than enough, but at other times, she wished for what Tesha had. A lover and a companion.

She removed her apron and gave the space one last look-over before heading out the door. The day was nice enough that she didn't mind walking the three blocks home. She'd left her car for Kayce to use.

Jensen stood under a tree, his cell phone to his ear. From the way he waved his free arm in the air, it was obvious the conversation was not a good one. He kicked at a rock and jammed the cell phone in his pant pockets. When she neared, his eyes widened in surprise. "Hello, Cassie Tucker."

She braced for the insult. "Mr. Ford." Cassie nodded at him and kept walking.

"Where you headed?" He came up alongside. "Don't you have a car?"

"I let my brother borrow it. He's staying with me until he leaves, for a few weeks in Myrtle Beach and then to college."

"You can borrow mine." He never ceased to perplex her. "If you don't mind driving a car that belongs to someone you don't like."

So her jab had bothered him. "No, thank you. And it would be easier to like you if you didn't keep insulting me."

Hands in his pockets, he remained quiet for a few moments.

Cassie let out a breath. "You seemed to be arguing earlier. Someone mad at you?"

"It was Adam. Tesha called him about something I did." He frowned and ducked his head.

She knew exactly what the call had been about. The night with Vanessa. But decided to have fun with him. "What did you do?"

His wide shoulders moved up and down. "Nothin'."

"Then Adam was wrong to be mad at you for doing nothing." She pressed her lips together to keep from smiling.

"He was right about the things he said."

"Sometimes I wish I had close knit family. I have a younger half-brother who I try hard to connect with, but he's a teenager and all into himself. Which is normal, I suppose. I wonder what it's like to have that connection with your parents and siblings," Cassie admitted.

Jensen slid a glance at her. "It can be a pain, too."

"Why are you out and about and not filming?" She changed the subject. Hadn't meant to get into her family dynamics.

"Headed that way in a bit, had to come into town to pick up some things for the weekend." His vague reply was accompanied by a scowl. "I'm going…" He stopped and looked around as if he'd not noticed where they were headed. "This is a cool spot."

Cassie agreed. The street was line with wooden Victorian-style homes. Different gingerbread accents decorated porches filled with ferns and rockers; it made Eleanor Street a place she was proud to come home to. With trees lining the sidewalks, the neighborhood was reminiscent of an older, gentler time.

"My house." She pointed to a green bungalow home. Not sure why, but she sensed Jensen needed some time to relax. "Wanna come in and meet my brother? He'll be thrilled." She held out a hand as if to stop him. "But you don't have to, of course."

"Sure." He went up the porch steps ahead of her.

Just two minutes later, Cassie made tea, listening to Kayce pelt Jensen with questions while they played a video game of some sort. Gunfire rang out and she shook her head at the combination of chatter, car engines and her wind chimes outside.

She poured two glasses of sweet tea and brought them to the living room. She sat on a chair opposite them. "What are y'all playing?"

Kayce barely looked up from the screen. "Grand Theft Auto."

"Sounds intense."

Both ignored her and then yelled in unison over something that happened, which of course she didn't understand.

Finally she gave up, reached for her Kindle and began reading.

JENSEN TRIED TO ignore her. Cassie had her long legs over the arm of an overstuffed chair, her hair up in a messy bun, in bare feet. A picture of absolute normalcy. She reached for her cup of tea and looked to him. Their eyes met for just an instant before he returned his attention to the game.

Adam had called him an idiot and chastised him for sleeping with Vanessa. Funny, since his brother had slept with her, too. It wasn't as if he was in a relationship. Single man could do as he pleased.

His cell vibrated in his pocket. Mark was probably having a fit that he'd taken off. But he needed to get away from the shoot. Vanessa was acting all grabby-feely and the crew kept snickering and making snide remarks. Usually it wasn't a big deal, but for some reason it had irritated him to the point of throwing a glass across the room and stomping out.

Now they had one more thing to pick on him about. Damn, they weren't like a bunch of high schoolers at times.

"You're dead." Cassie's brother gave him a "you suck at gaming" look. "That wasn't even hard."

"Yeah. I got distracted." He put the controller down. "Gotta go."

"Can I get a picture with you?" It was obvious from the redness in the boy's cheeks, he'd been building up the courage to ask.

"Of course. I want one, too." Jensen positioned himself to the side and took one with his phone.

"I'll be right back." Kayce stood and rushed to his room.

Cassie studied him. "You look more relaxed after killing people or whatever it is you did."

"Yeah, but I better get back to the shoot." He stood and posed for several pictures with her brother, who immediately lost interest in him and hurried away, his thumbs flying over the cell phone keys.

"You made his day. Thank you." Cassie went with him to the door. "Sometimes you can be okay." Her smile warmed him, and Jensen lowered his eyelids and made his perfected ambivalent look.

"It was cool. Thanks for the tea. Later." He gave her a two-fingered salute and jogged down the stairs.

Damn, if he didn't feel better. Just those few hours away from the crew and prying eyes re-energized him. He made it back to his motorcycle, climbed on and headed back to face his agent.

Two more days and then Cabo.

He pushed thoughts of a weekend with Vanessa away. The thought of spending the night with her held little enticement. She was fun to be around with and hopefully that would enough for them. Although they'd share a room, he'd ask for two beds and would insist they sleep separately.

CADEN WAITED FOR him at the house, and he wondered if his brother's visit had more to do with him or Cassie. Of course he had no right to feel any type of propriety over her. Truth be told, she and Caden were probably a better match. Both lived normal lives, and Caden had a lot more in common with Cassie than he did.

His brother sat and watched while Mark ranted about how Jensen was setting production back by disappearing twice now.

The producers jumped in with some blah blah about budgets. Jensen assumed an apologetic expression while assuring them he'd not pull anymore disappearing acts. He offered to cancel the trip to Cabo, but the execs wouldn't have it.

"Everything is in place," Mark snapped. "We can't change it now. Just make sure you put in the time to make up for ghosting on us."

Jensen nodded in agreement and looked to Caden, who shrugged in return. Now was not the time to allow his brother to pull him into some sort of trouble. Caden had the look in his eye that told of getting into something that could send the movie execs into comas.

"Guess what?" Caden neared when the suits finally walked off assured he'd do his part.

Jensen held still so the makeup artist, Chachi, could do his thing. "What?"

"Undercover assignment. Tonight at strip joint."

"I'm in." Jensen grinned and stopped when the makeup artist tilted his chin up. "I want to be an undercover John."

"No, you can't." Caden gave him an incredulous look. "You're too easily recognizable."

"Then why are you telling me if I can't be part of if."

"You are the distraction." Caden cleared his throat when the make-up artist glared at him.

Chachi wagged a make up brush at his brother. "Did you not hear the tongue lashing he just got? If he goes to a strip bar, he won't make it to early call in the morning."

"Yeah. I will." Surely he'd not be out that late. "How late we talkin'?"

Caden shrugged. "I'll have you back in time for early call. What time is that?"

"Seven."

"Six." Chachi corrected and winked at Caden. "He has to be in this chair at six," he said, pronouncing the words "theese" and "share."

"Wow. That's early," Caden gave him a worried look. "But

yeah, I'll have you here by then."

THAT NIGHT HE walked into the Nashville police station. The usual smell of sweat, coffee and old building reminded him of his brother. Although not glamorous, he sometimes envied Caden's calling. A police officer looked up from his desk and did a double take. He prepared for the inevitable "aren't you Jensen Ford?"

Instead the guy looked over his shoulder. "Ford, your brother's here." He promptly went back to whatever he was doing on his computer, looking at a pile of citations on his desk.

He'd forgotten, the men in blue had more important things on their minds.

"Oh. My. God." What could have been a man in drag, grabbed his arm. Handcuffed hands wrapped around Jensen's arm in a two-handed vice grip. "You are so hot." With a sigh, the person leaned against his side. "Smell good too baby."

Jensen looked around expecting to be rescued, but the arresting officer just rolled his eyes and walked to his desk to grab a set of keys.

Caden walked up and looked at his new arm attachment. "Gigi, you in trouble again?"

The drag queen shrugged and once again laid his greasy head on Jensen. "This time it was worth it. Why didn't you tell me you had a famous brother? All these years we've been so tight, and you didn't share."

"We have not been tight." Caden attempted to pry the person off of Jensen. "Come on, Gigi. Let the man go."

"I don't want to go to jail. I didn't do anything that bad."

Jensen could feel his eyes getting rounder. If Gigi started crying, all the makeup would end up on him.

"Don't make him cry," he said to Caden, only to garner a narrow-eyed look from his new admirer.

"I'm Gigi. I'm a her," *she* snapped and pushed away. An officer neared and unlocked her from the chair. "Come on Gigi, let's get you into a nice cozy cell."

Gigi glared at Jensen. "Dumbass."

The tall wide-shouldered woman teetered away on her heels, following the officer who walked with slow patience alongside. "I better get my own cell."

"Ready?" Caden smiled at him as Jensen brushed at his jacket sleeve. "Gigi didn't leave any cooties. You'll live."

Jensen wasn't too sure about the cooties. But the giant woman, had some strong perfume.

They went out to Caden's jeep, and he looked over the dark blue vehicle. Caden had added a few enhancements to his birthday present. They walked around it as his younger brother pointed out the new light bar and speaker system. It had been lifted and sported a wench in the front.

"Nice." Jensen had to grin at his brother's enthusiasm when it came to the vehicle. "What about the Jag? You ever drive it?"

Caden scratched at the stubble on his chin. "Yeah. On the weekends, sometimes. If Cassie accepts a date, I'm gonna drive it."

"She's off limits."

"Says who?"

He didn't bother answering because it would be a lie.

"You aren't thinking of seducing her, are you?" Caden

neared, his nostrils flared. "I'll kick your ass if you do. She's a nice girl."

"Not that it's any of your business, but no, I have no plans to sleep with her. I'm seeing my costar. Heading to Cabo this weekend."

Caden let out a whistle. "She's hot."

"Yep. Now what do I have to do at this strip joint?"

His brother seemed to have second thoughts. "You sure this won't be bad for your reputation?"

"I'm a bad boy. Bad boys go to strip clubs."

Several hours later, the blue lights from all the cop cars, parked askew in all directions, were blinding. Jensen leaned against his car and watched Caden, and several other undercover guys dragged men to patrol cars. When someone took a swing at Caden, Jensen almost rushed into defend his little brother. But Caden took the man down with one swift move and handcuffed him in seconds.

All right, so the boy could take care of himself. It didn't mean Jensen could help wanting to kick the asshole on the ground.

"Thanks for the help." Caden finally came over, a wide grin on his face. "Now I can spend the rest of the week writing up reports."

Jensen nodded. "The exciting life of a cop."

"It comes in spurts." Caden touched his bottom lip gingerly. "Don't want Momma to see this. She'll have a fit."

Jensen studied his brother's bruised lip. "He clocked you good."

"Got lucky."

Across the street, a twenty-four-hour diner with bright neon signs and even brighter interior was almost empty. "Wanna grab a bite before I head back?"

"Sure. Hold on a sec." Caden went to where his partner waited.

Seconds later he returned. "Come on. They make a killer Reuben."

Chapter Nine

IN TESHA'S LARGE kitchen, Cassie stretched, thankful the morning went off without a hitch. With most of the dishes cleared, Cassie's mind was already on what needed to be done at her shop. When her phone rang, Cassie answered without looking at the display. When Nick's voice sounded in her ear, it gave her a new reason to dislike Mondays. She really had to start checking the damn thing to see who called.

"You promised to call me back." He didn't sound put off or upset, but rather resigned. "Did you forget?"

"I umm…yes, I did." She eyed the people who lingered after breakfast. It was time for her to help Tesha finish up and head to her cupcake shop. Although the extra money from helping feed the film crew was great, it was exhausting keeping up with both it and her shop.

"…I am coming to see you. We need to talk," Nick was saying. She'd stopped listening when Jensen strolled in and poured coffee into a cup. Then without more than a quick head tip, he went to sit next to Vanessa, who continued a conversation with the agent and producer, not bothering to acknowledge him.

"What?" Cassie moved to stand in the hallway. "There is no reason for you to come here. What is so important, we can't discuss over the phone?"

"It's not something I can tell you over the phone. Go to dinner with me."

Nick Madison had been her life for almost four years. Cassie had a flashback of walking in on him rockin' and rollin' with her friend.

"No Nick. I don't want to."

"I'll be there this evening. Just hear me out."

He hung up and she let her arm fall to her side. "Argh!"

"Who was that? Is Kayce all right?" Tesha came and touched her shoulder.

Cassie let out a huff. "That was my ex. He keeps insisting on coming to talk to me. I don't want to see him."

"Why now?" Tesha gave her a worried look. "Hasn't it been years since you broke up?"

"Yes, over two years." Cassie pushed away from the wall. "I need to finish cleaning up and head to town. Can I come back here afterwards? I don't want him to find me if he does come into town."

"Of course."

For some reason, she burst into tears and rushed to the laundry room behind the kitchen.

Tesha was on her heels. "Honey, it's going to be okay. Don't worry about it. He won't bother you. I can call Deputy Castro and ask him to keep an eye out."

"Its not just that. I'm being silly." Cassie wiped at her face and managed a wobbly smile.

"That time of the month." That and seeing pictures of Jensen and Vanessa in Cabo over the weekend. Hugging and kissing while swimming or lounging in the sun. According to the entertainment show, they had tried to hide but were discovered after a hotel staff member let it slip.

She felt so stupid for having a crush on a celebrity to the point of crying. What a fool she was turning out to be. Angry, she cried harder.

Tesha patted her shoulder. "Don't cry. It's going to be okay. Hey I know. Why don't you call the lady that fills in for you in the mornings and ask if she can stay the rest day?. You need a break."

"I can...can't afford to do that." Once again she burst into tears and then stomped her foot. "Why in the hell can't I stop crying?"

"What's wrong?" Jensen peered at her from the doorway. "Something happen?" His gaze bore into hers and now she wished for the ground to open up and swallow her.

"I'm hurt, angry, broke and sad. Oh and let's not forget, I'm on my period. My life sucks today. Something neither of you get right now."

She stormed away from a shocked Tesha and rounded Jensen. "I'll be back later, Tesha." She turned to her friend. "I'm sorry."

She made it to her car and sunk into the seat, a glob of bird poop plopped onto the windshield. She giggled, hiccupped and opened the window. "Why don't you crap on my head too while you're at it. Little fucker."

She closed the window and stared at the steering wheel. "I'm going crazy. I need to be locked up." She jumped when Jensen opened the passenger door and got in.

He tapped on her shoulder. "I can loan you some money."

Cassie burst into laughter. She laughed until her eyes watered. Then looked at his confused face and laughed even harder.

"Or not." He didn't move but watched her with interest. "Things must be pretty bad. You're a mess."

"Yes I am. I am a mess. And you know what? I need to pull up my big girl panties and deal with it. This is not who I am. I'm not a crier and I'm not a mean person."

She made to shoo him with both hands. "If you will excuse me, I'll be on my way. Thank you for your offer, but I'm not really broke. Not sure why I said that other than a moment of menstrual insanity." A giggle erupted and his eyes widened.

"Oh, that."

"Yes that. I'll talk to you later, Jensen. Now shoo. Your girlfriend is probably wondering where you're off to."

"You saw the entertainment news, then," he stated in a flat voice.

"Yep you two looked very good. It's probably great you tanned your ass."

"It was not…" He stopped talking when she started the car.

"See you later, Jensen. I really have to go. No telling what emotion will bust free next."

"Let's go for a walk." He leaned back into the seat and looked straight out the front windshield. "Come on. I dare you to do something crazy."

"Crazy? I think I've got that covered." Cassie couldn't help peeking at her reflection in the side view mirror. "I don't want to go for a walk. That's cr…"

"Crazy?"

"All right, fine." She opened the door and walked around her clunker. "Where are we going?"

Back hunched, she knew her face was tear streaked and her

hair a mess. At the moment she didn't care. He was dating Vanessa Morgan, multi-million dollar a film actress who always looked like a magazine ad.

Her attention was captivated when he stuck a long leg out, dusty boot first and straightened to full height. Sunglasses in place, she could not tell where he looked so she turned to study the roadside. "Which way?"

"Come on." He turned toward Adam's house. "How about a quick stroll through the woods?"

It was on the tip of her tongue to remind him that most of the trees had been chopped down thanks to the film production, but instead she caught up with him. "I'm not in a good mood. I don't want to argue."

"Is that what you think will happen?" He continued past the house through the sparse trees. "It's already been established you don't like me. What can we possibly argue about?"

Instead of replying she looked around and noticed that the leaves were beginning to change. Why had she not noticed it before? Too preoccupied with all the stuff of life, she'd missed the changing of seasons. Her favorite time of year approached. She slid a gaze to Jensen. He didn't have the normal worries, of course. Everything was taken care of for him. There was no way a mega star like Jensen Ford could relate with what she dealt with. Fine, so he tried to take her mind off her near nervous breakdown, and although it was a nice gesture, it was only a matter of time before he'd say or do something stupid and hurt her feelings again.

There was also the added fact that he was one of the reasons she'd lost her composure back at the house. Cassie let out a sigh. "So, you and Vanessa, huh?"

He turned to her and lifted a shoulder. "Yeah."

Her stomach tumbled and she couldn't help letting out a breath. "It seems like it happens a lot. Costars hooking up."

"Tell me about it." Jensen stopped and looked up at a tree where an owl sat on a branch studying him in return. "Check that out."

Cassie studied the man instead. Wearing his usual black t-shirt and jeans, he was perfect. Tussled hair, aviators and muscular. With his hands on his hips, he seemed to be posing for a glamour shot. He and the owl stared at each other and Jensen laughed. "He is really interested in us."

"Don't you think it's sort of creepy?" Cassie looked to the other trees to ensure there weren't more, gathering to attack.

"Nah. He's kinda cute." Jensen made hooting sounds, and the owl remained silent. "I think he likes me."

"Well, why wouldn't he? Everyone loves you."

He lowered his glasses, and the clear green eyes met hers. "You don't. Which I'm sure is a mistake, deep down inside you find me irresistible. You got that single woman repression going on."

"You're a pompous ass." Cassie headed back to her car. "I don't know why I fall for it every time." She growled when he took her arm and turned her to him.

"I was kidding. Why are you wound so tight?"

If only he didn't stand so close. "I told you, I'm not in a good mood."

"You definitely are in a state. Wanna go eat ice cream? There's some in Adam's house. Isn't that what women do when it's that time?"

This time she couldn't help a giggle. "You really can't help it, can you?"

"What?" He frowned down at her.

"Saying the dumbest things. I need to go to town. Got cupcakes to bake."

Jensen walked alongside seeming relaxed. "What about the ice cream?"

"When woman eat the ice cream, in this state." She made quotation marks with her fingers. "they eat it alone in the dark in front of the television wearing fat clothes and messy hair. We prefer to be bundled up in a blanket with a cat and don't want any witnesses to the sloppy mess we've become."

"Oh."

"Thanks for the offer, anyway."

They walked back until in front of the movie trailers and parted ways, he to Adam's house and she back to the car, which of course didn't start when she turned the key in the ignition. "Just kill me." Too mentally exhausted to get out of the car, Cassie slumped forward and dialed Tesha's number.

"I need to borrow your truck."

THAT NIGHT SHE sat in front of the television watching a Lifetime movie. Her ice cream of choice was caramel swirl, and she washed it down with a water glass half filled with merlot. The doorbell rang and she didn't bother moving. Whoever it was would hopefully go away.

She'd told Tesha she'd lock herself in and would be fine. After texting Nick and telling him she was not going to be home, she was sure he'd not drive out. Now she stared at the door and held her breath praying he'd not ignored her request.

"Cassie? Why didn't you open the door? Had me worried for a minute." Mrs. Miller, the hardware store owner and dear friend, came in through the back door. "Thank God I have a key."

The older woman took the ice cream and spoon from her hands and tasted it. "Pretty good stuff."

Then she walked away with it and her wine. "But what you need is some good soup."

Cassie's mouth fell open. "No, I'm pretty sure I want the ice cream."

"What you want, and need are not always the same." Mrs. Miller called out from the kitchen. "I brought my famous orzo spinach soup." She returned with a tray. On it two bowls of hearty soup, two chunks of bread and bottle of sparkling water.

It smelled delicious. "I wish you were my mother." Cassie sat up and pulled an oversized book on her lap to rest the bowl on. "You take the tray."

They ate in silence for a bit watching a movie with a predictable story line.

Finally Mrs. Miller spoke. "Tesha called me. She was worried about you. Told me you had a prize-winning hissy fit. What bothers you the most, honey?"

"I'm not sure. Everything is battling for first place," Cassie admitted. "Between the shop barely making it, my car issues and helping Kayce get all he needs for college, it's overwhelming."

Her eyes burned as she neared the edge of crying again. "Its silly, really. God has been so good, I got the job with the movie company working at Tesha's, and one of the movie execs has set me up to cater cupcakes to a party his wife is throwing in Nashville next month."

"I understand." Mrs. Miller studied her. "You are all work and no play. It's too much, and although you are strong, right now you have a lot on your plate. You deserve a night of this." She pointed to her pajamas and the television.

The movie credits ended, and she turned it to the entertainment channel. "You know what? You're right. After the movie stuff is over, I'm going to treat myself to a week of vacation. Maybe go to the beach."

"Now you're talking." Mrs. Miller put her feet up next to hers on the coffee table. "Maybe you'll meet Mr. Cassie."

They laughed and Cassie couldn't help wondering what Jensen would do if he spent a week at the beach. Being he lived in Los Angeles, he probably didn't think much about it. "I'd like to meet someone nice."

"Adam's brothers are all single." Mrs. Miller wagged her eyebrows. "And that cameraman, the one that looks like Matt Damon, is also unattached. He told Debbie he was looking for a good woman."

Mrs. Miller and her two lady friends, Debbie and Carol, helped at Tesha's in the afternoons and were forever stalking the actors and crew.

"He does look like Matt Damon, doesn't he?" Cassie avoided remarking on the Ford brothers. "I thought he was seeing Vanessa, but it looks like she and Jensen are an item now."

"Oh, I doubt that. Those boys wouldn't dare bring that floozy around their momma."

"Mrs. Miller!" Cassie had to laugh at the woman's comment. "I'm sure as good looking as the Ford brothers are, they've dated plenty of those types."

"Dated. But never married or brought them home." Mrs. Miller gave her a firm nod as if she knew it to be true. "Miriam Ford will send a floozy like that Vanessa packing."

"Well let's just admit that all of the Ford men are way out of my league." Cassie sipped her water and watched as actresses walked a red carpet turning this way and that for the paparazzi.

Cassie motioned to the television with her glass. "That, there, is their league."

"Sticks in glittery dresses." Mrs. Miller huffed and stood with the bowls in her hands. "Besides, the way Jensen Ford watches you, I'm surprised he's not asked you out yet."

She didn't dare admit the kiss to Mrs. Miller, but the actor would not stoop so low as to be seen in public on a date with her. "Yeah well, I think he likes to find creative ways to annoy me."

"Boys do that when they like girls."

Cassie snorted. "But it all changes after elementary school."

The doorbell rang and before she could stop her, Mrs. Miller opened the door to reveal a Nick holding a bouquet of roses.

"Well, hello, young man. Come in out of the cold." She took the flowers from him. "Let me put these in water. I'm afraid Cassie is a bit under the weather. You may want to keep your distance."

Nick looked to her and for once Cassie was glad for her messy hair and lack of make up. "Sorry, I should have called again, but my cell phone is dead. I need to go to the store tomorrow to get a replacement. I dropped it into the toilet."

"Oh dear. Sit down." Mrs. Miller placed a bottle of water into his hand. "I'm Tellulah Miller. A friend of Cassie's."

Nick stuck out his hand. "Nick Madison, Cassie's friend from Nashville. Came to check on my girl."

"Well, aren't you sweet. I'll be on my way then."

"Please stay." Cassie attempted to find a way to let the woman know she didn't want to be alone with him, but Mrs. Miller had bustled into the kitchen and called out. "Don't be silly. You can tell Nick all about the movie."

She stuck her head out and looked to Nick. "Don't tire her, she needs to rest."

"Yes Ma'am." Nick gave her his best-practiced smile. The smile that made prospective mother-in-laws and clients trust him. To this day, her mother swore Cassie overreacted about him actually having sex with another woman. Or imagined the entire thing.

After Mrs. Miller left, Cassie got up and poured a glass of wine, not offering Nick any. She plopped back down on the couch. "What is so important, you had to tell me in person?"

For a long moment, he studied her face. "You are so beautiful. I can't believe I let you go."

Cassie fidgeted under his scrutiny. "Well it happened, and we've moved on."

"I didn't."

Of all the times for him to come crawling back, this was the worst timing. Although she'd dreamed of it many times. Of how she'd look down her perfectly made-up nose, a hand on her slender hip, because of course, in her imagination, she'd lost twenty pounds, while she'd tell him to take a hike. But for some reason instead of feeling satisfaction, she felt pity.

"It's been years. Let's not even try to act as if you cared for me."

"I loved you in my own way. But I was so stupid. Such an idiot." He inhaled. "I'm just going to come out and say it."

Cassie swallowed and waited for him to tell her he wanted to work things out. She had a practiced speech, a stern but gentle way to let him down.

"I need your forgiveness for having wronged you in such a way. I ruined our wedding plans. A day that should have been our happiest, I sullied the sacred occasion. For that and for hurting you, I ask that you please forgive me." His eyes were shiny, and she wondered if he was about to cry.

"There was no wedding day to ruin. I've accepted it and although it was a horrible way to end things. I do forgive you. But you could have said all of this to me over the phone. I would have told you I forgave you a long time ago."

"That not the only thing I want to ask of you."

"Nick, please…" She took a long drink.

"Listen to me." Nick moved to sit next to her on the couch. "It's important that you understand."

At his serious expression her stomach pitched. Something was wrong. "What is it?"

"I'm dying."

Chapter Ten

"**G**ET YOUR HEAD out of the clouds, Jensen," the director called out. "That was crap!"

Through the fog of cold medication, he tried to get mad, but the guy was right. He'd woken up with a head cold, and although he'd powered through most of the morning, at this point, he could barely keep from puking. And, of course, today was the day they shot fight scenes and a confrontation with his arch nemesis.

He made eye contact with the older actor who in return gave him a sympathetic look. "Sorry. Feel like shit."

"Power through it. I have a flight tomorrow I refuse to miss." The man lifted an eyebrow.

So much for sympathy.

"I NEED MY mom," Jensen said into the phone that night as he lay bundled in his bed surrounded by medication, bottles of water and a box of tissues.

His mother's voice soothed in his ear. "I'm sorry you're sick, honey. Ask someone to make you some tea."

No one was around; every person in the crew, including his fake girlfriend, was giving him wide berth as most of them had other "pressing" engagements they didn't want to miss if they caught his cold.

"Yeah, I'll get the butler to bring it immediately."

His mother laughed. "What about Cassie? Is she nearby? Ask if she can bring you something?"

"Last time I saw her she was in the middle of a nervous breakdown. Something about menstrual emotions."

There was silence for a moment. Yep, he'd done something anti-woman by her huff. "Being emotional is not a nervous breakdown, honey. She probably needed you to just hug her."

"I took her for a walk. Then she got mad again."

"It's a wonder you manage to date at all, Jensen. Sometimes I worry you'll never marry and end up a dirty old man. With dyed hair and a face lift, chasing twenty-year-olds."

"Ewww."

"Good night, honey. Get some tea."

He let the phone fall to the bed and decided to take his mother's advice. After two rings, Cassie surprised him by answering. He'd not seen her in the last three days. Instead of going to Tesha's bed and breakfast in the mornings, he'd stayed in Adam's house eating cereal and drinking coffee.

Filming was at a crucial place, and he had a lot of lines to memorize.

"Hello?" Her voice brought him to the present. "Jensen?"

"Hi." He sneezed and tried again. "Hey how are you?"

"I'm….good."

He tried to remember why he called, the sound of her voice brought images of huge whiskey-colored eyes and long waves of honey brown hair. "Are you feeling better?"

"Yes. I am great. You sound funny."

"I have a cold."

She was silent for a few minutes. "I'm sorry you don't feel well." Jensen wasn't sure how to respond to the soft sounds of her breathing. "It's hard to work while sick."

"It's not so bad." He sneezed and blew his nose. "Sorry."

The line went dead. She'd hung up on him. Great.

The bed dipped and Jensen opened his eyes to see Cassie hovering over him. "You look horrible."

"I feel worse." He coughed and waved her away. "You need to keep your distance. You don't want to catch this."

Cassie placed a cup of tea on the nightstand and grabbed his arms. "Sit up. I have a strong constitution, rarely get sick."

She put the cup in his hands and went to the window and lifted it open. Then she grabbed a trashcan and threw all the tissues away. "Why isn't anyone here? I can't believe they left you here alone."

"We're behind schedule. They are shooting around me until I don't look like death warmed over. They checked on me this morning and decided I needed to stay in bed." He coughed again. "Where have you been? I haven't seen you in about a week."

A slight frown marred her smooth brow. "Things are a bit complicated for me right now." She smiled a bit too cheerfully. "The good news is my brother has gone to college." The heaviness in the air made him wonder what the other complication was. From experience it usually meant a person of the opposite sex.

"I appreciate the tea, but you didn't have to."

"I know." She moved with brisk efficiency and left the room. A few moments later Cassie returned with a bowl of soup. "I can't take credit for this. I bought it at the diner. They make the best chicken and vegetable."

While he ate, she sat in a chair, chin in her hand looking absently out the window.

Jensen didn't want to know, but he asked anyway. "So what are the complications about?"

He wasn't sure what he saw in her gaze, something between longing and sadness. "Nothing that won't fix itself, just need to wait. Unfortunately, I'm not a patient person. Once the filming wraps up next week, I'll have more time to do other things. Take care of an ill friend and devote more time to my shop."

Before he could ask more questions, she jumped to her feet and took the bowl. She motioned to the nightstand with her chin. "Take those pills. If I ever get sick, it's the only thing that makes me get better."

He did while she watched.

"There now. I'll let you rest." She cocked her head to the side. "I do believe this is the first time we've been around each other without some sort of insult flying."

After she left he lifted his cell phone. A text from Caden buzzed. *"Hey Bro. C U tonight."*

What the heck was happening that night? He looked at the date, it didn't help. Finally he pushed the call button. "Hey," Caden answered. "You ready?"

"For what?" Jensen grabbed a tissue and blew his nose.

"Isn't the crew party tonight?" He could hear voices in the background. "Some of the guys want to come."

"Yeah, that's cool. I won't be there. I'm sick."

"Can I still go?"

Jensen hung up after assuring Caden that he and his cop friends were invited. He fell back onto the pillows and wondered if he should call Cassie and thank her. Or better yet, go to her house in person and thank her. Or maybe send flowers. He looked up and saw Mark leaning on the doorframe.

"What the hell is up with all this sick shit. You need to get better by tomorrow. We need some candid shots of you and Vanessa. I tried to convince her to come over here, but she slammed the door in my face. Everyone has gone crazy around here."

"Can you bring me some juice?"

"Hell no, I'm not stepping inside that den of disease." Mark walked away.

BY THE END of the next day, Jensen felt like a new man. He walked to Tesha's house, intent on finding a good meal. The women who worked in the afternoons usually left hearty fare for them.

Once inside the house he was shocked to find only Cassie. Tesha's jazzy music played from somewhere in the background, and Cassie stood in the kitchen, her back to him, swaying with a glass of wine in her hand. The scent of Italian herbs made his stomach grumble, but he didn't dare interrupt.

For a few moments he stood there and watched, enjoying a rare moment where she seemed to be free of the usual nervousness that seemed to surround her. Her long hair swayed as she did whatever it was at the stove. Then she put the glass down beside it and lifted both arms in the air and twirled.

"Oh shit." She stumbled forward and steadied herself on the countertop. "You scared the crap out of me."

The tension was back.

A soft blush colored her cheeks, and she frowned at him. "You look better. Need something to eat?"

"Yes." He was full of words today. "Please."

"You're in luck. I'm making spaghetti."

After pouring himself a glass of water, he went to the table. "Where's everyone at?"

"Some of the guys are in their trailers. They are watching a game. The rest of the production crew went to town for some kind of celebration."

She placed bread in a basket in the middle of the table and two heaping bowls of pasta. "It's nothing fancy." Cassie sat to his left and began to eat, her eyes focused on the view through the large French doors.

It was pleasant to share a meal there with her. Not in a noisy restaurant or surrounded by the crew. The spaghetti was simple, but delicious.

"It's good." Once again his ability to convey his feelings astounded him. "So you're not just a great baker, but a good cook too."

"Thanks."

"Why are you here and not home?"

"Tesha is gone to Nashville. Mrs. Miller and the ladies can't come in the morning. Instead of getting up super early with a car that may or may not start, I figured I'd spend the night."

"Why don't you get your car fixed? I hear the garage in town is good."

Cassie let out a slow breath. "It needs a new starter. Before, I couldn't afford the expense. Now I just don't have the time. I can't function without a car until after this movie wraps up. I'll get it fixed then. The poor thing needs an oil change and new tires too. Once that is done, it will be in great shape." She chuckled. "At least that's what I keep telling myself."

Her grin made his stomach tumble. Damn if he wasn't falling for this woman.

The idea shook him, and it was Jensen's turn to study the view outside. The leaves were changing; the autumn colors reminded him of Cassie's eyes and hair. His favorite time of year, when the humidity lowered, and he could ride for miles without sweating to death in his helmet.

"I'll take a look at it."

"What?" Cassie stared at him as if he's just spoken Japanese. "You don't have time."

THEY'D BARELY FINISHED eating when Jensen jumped up and headed outside. Before Cassie could stop the maniac, she was chasing him to her car. He'd nipped the keys from the counter and, with a sense of purpose, gone outside.

He jumped into the passenger seat of her car and turned the ignition. Of course the damn thing started; he motioned for her to move away and drove toward Adam's house next door. He pulled the car into driveway and strolled to the garage before she could catch up.

"What the hell are you doing?" She watched as he grabbed several tools with the efficiency of a man who knew what he was doing.

Without answering her, he made his way to her car and opened the hood, which he must have popped before getting out.

"Jensen, please don't make things worse than they already are. I need this car."

He looked up at her, his hazel eyes bright. "I know what I'm doing. For years most weekends I worked on cars with Dad."

"That was how many years ago?" She put her hands on her hips and tapped her foot.

An hour later, her mouth fell open as her car started, and not only that, but the engine also purred like it was new. Jensen wiped his hands with a rag and leaned in the window, his face too close. "Just needed a few adjustments. It should get you back and forth safely until you get time to take it to the shop. You will need a new starter soon, but I think it's not that bad."

"Now how about you reward me with dessert?" His eyes locked on her mouth, and she understood the ill-hidden message.

"I have some cupcakes back at Tesha's."

He motioned for her to drive. "I'll walk over."

God, what was he doing? He constantly changed from one moment to the next, from a total asshole to an endearing guy who fixed her car. At any given moment, he was a mega star, then switched without notice to just a guy.

It was too confusing, hard to figure out who would walk into her world when. As attracted as she was to him, in her mind, she knew that being in Jensen's world was a very dangerous and potentially devastating thing. Why was he coming over now? It wasn't a good idea, not at all.

She entered and made a beeline for her wine. Her hands shook as she lifted her glass to drink. Time alone with Jensen was not a good idea. Especially right now.

So many emotions tumbling around in her head. For one thing, she owed Nick an answer. He'd asked her to move back to Nashville and spend the last months with him. Not that she owed it to him, but he only had a brother for family.

Yes, he had parents, cliché rich parents who'd shipped him off to boarding school for most of his life and hired someone for whatever else was needed.

At the sound of the door opening, she tensed. "Something's got your brow furrowed again. You think too much, Cassie Tucker." Jensen lifted her chin and peered into her eyes.

He was going to kiss her. In her gut she knew this kiss would change many things.

He cupped her face with both hands and held it as his lips took hers. The kiss was soft, gentle, almost as if he were afraid to hurt her. Cassie slid her hands up his sides and splayed them on his back enjoying the feel of his hard muscles under her palms.

When he pulled her closer against him, Cassie let go and allowed Jensen to consume her totally. The feel of his hard planes against her softer ones, the large arms surrounding her and the smell of him, some sort of expensive cologne, melted the last morsels of reserve.

She parted her lips for him, took his tongue into her mouth and suckled at it while snaking her arms around his neck and weaving her fingers through his silky hair to pull him closer, unable to get enough of him.

"I want you so much, Cassie." His heated whisper in her ear was like an elixir. She could barely stand the barrier of clothing between them. "Since the first moment I saw you, I knew you could be my undoing."

His trailed his tongue from her earlobe to the side of her neck, while she clung to him in desperation. "Oh, God. You are an amazing kisser."

There was a twinkle in his eyes when they met hers. "Then kiss me again. Take me."

He leaned forward but did not touch his lips to hers. Instead, he waited for her to take the initiative. Cassie pulled his head down and covered his mouth with hers. Tasting and prodding until he let her move in. With a soft growl that came from the base of his throat, he cupped her bottom and pulled her against his hardness.

Jensen was hard, erect and wonderful. He ground into her very hot and super ready center.

If someone had told her it was possible to climax just from making out she would have laughed. But at this moment, she began to float. Cassie kissed him harder, a moan escaping when he shifted just enough to grind against her once again.

"Mmmm." She gasped when he bit the side of her neck. "Yes."

"Oh, shit. Excuse me." The voice was like a bucket of cold water. Cassie shoved Jensen away barely able to contain her hard breathing enough to identify who'd walked in.

Jensen turned to block her from the intruder. His large body in front of hers, but she could see he breathed just as hard. "Hey, Mike. The party over?"

Somehow his demeanor as well as the tone of his voice remained even, as if it was no big deal that the man had practically walked in on them making love.

Cassie skirted around them and went to the kitchen counter, attempting to find something to busy herself with until they left, and she could lock the door.

Mike, the cameraman looked over his shoulder then back to Jensen. "We shoot early in the morning. Over on the empty field. I was sent to find you and tell you to be ready at five."

"Not a problem." Jensen walked towards her, a curve to his lips. He opened his mouth as if to say something, but then stopped.

Vanessa walked through the doors. From the flush of color on her face, she'd been drinking quite a bit. Or maybe not much given the woman barely ate. "There you are. Why didn't you come out with us?" She walked straight to Jensen and draped herself easily around him. "Miss me?"

The perfect ending to her evening. For some stupid reason, she'd assumed they'd hooked up once and were no longer an item. Why would Jensen come on to her and kiss her otherwise?

As if noticing her for the first time, Vanessa looked to her. "Hi there. Cassie, right?"

"Errr.... yeah. I'm going to bed. Help yourselves to anything you want."

Cassie did not make eye contact with Jensen or Mike, instead looking at Vanessa. "Have a good night."

The actress giggled and ran her finger along the side of Jensen's face. "Oh, I plan to."

"I'm gone two days, and all this happened?" Tesha sat at one of the tables in the cupcake shop working on specials sign, while Cassie piped decorations on her pumpkin cheesecake cupcakes.

"Nick wants you to move to Nashville?" Her friend gave her a questioning look. "And then you make out with Jensen and almost get busted by Vanessa? Good lord, girl, I can't move away, you'll hold up a bank or something."

In spite of the fact that the day before when she'd cried as soon as she found herself alone, today she could barely hold back a smile. "I can't believe it, either." She let out a deep sigh. "What am I going to do?"

"First of all, I don't think it's fair for Nick to want you to walk away from your life to take care of him. It's too much to ask. I think it's his way of getting you back. How do we know he's really dying?"

"I really don't think he'd go that far? Do you?" Cassie had to admit Nick looked healthy to her. But many times people with cancer didn't die right away and didn't look too bad until their last days.

"You probably never thought he was the type to sleep with another woman just before your wedding either?"

She pushed the finished tray aside. "True."

Tesha got up and poured two cups of coffee. "Now, about Jensen. I totally get why you're attracted to him. I mean, Adam is a hunk, but I have to admit of all the brothers Jensen is just freaking beautiful."

She frowned. "And although deep inside he is a good person, he's also a player. Adam says not to believe the tabloids, that Jensen is a one-woman man. Then again, last night proved otherwise."

The thought of Vanessa and Jensen together the night before made her want to throw something. "Yeah, I shouldn't have gone there with him."

"So is he a good kisser?" Tesha grinned and held her cup with both hands. "Spill it."

It was nice to find something to laugh about, after how bad and embarrassed she'd felt the night before.

"He is an amazing kisser."

Chapter Eleven

"I HEAR YOU fly out tonight." Jensen took a swig of his water while Vanessa dug through her purse, her brows drawn together.

"Finally, I'm so glad I can leave this po-dunk town," Vanessa exclaimed, uncoiling from the couch. "I'm so sick of all the cutesy crap, I could scream." She motioned around the room with her hand. "And the accents here are annoying. I'm glad you managed to get rid of yours."

He bit back a curse. "I can bring it back pretty damn quick," he drawled in his best Tennessee accent. "And you're talking about where I grew up."

"Sorry." She didn't look the least bit remorseful. "So," she looked to Mark, "where are Jensen and I going to rendezvous next?"

"Dinner at Lux, then you're going to be seen leaving her apartment." His manager looked from one to the other and then concentrated on Jensen. "Stay away from anyone else for now, especially a certain someone around here. Someone could get a picture."

Vanessa's eyes narrowed at Jensen. "Like, who exactly would he be interested in around here?"

"I'm just sayin'," Mark quipped, his eyes on the cell phone he held up. He wasn't fooling Jensen. The man had heard from the camera guy. He already knew what happened the night before with Cassie.

"Ha," Vanessa grabbed a nail file and held it up like a trophy. "I found it. Yay." She lounged back into the couch and looked up at him. "I'm off to Nashville in half an hour. Want to go with me?"

"Nope." Jensen turned to see that Cassie had joined Tesha in the kitchen. They held cups of coffee and watched the interaction between he, Mark, and Vanessa as if it were a television show.

Tesha lifted a hand to him. "Hi."

Cassie didn't make eye contact. She kept her gaze on Vanessa. "Have a safe trip."

The actress jumped to her feet and rushed to the women. "I'm going to miss your cooking, and Cassie, I'll be seeing you in LA next month."

"I'm sorry?" Cassie gave the actress a puzzled look. Jensen wondered what the hell Vanessa was talking about. Last night she didn't even remember Cassie's name.

Vanessa laughed. "You're funny. Or did I forget to tell you? You know, the Hollywood party. I told my girlfriend you'd provide the cupcakes. It's only going to be about five hundred people, but it will help get your name out."

The color drained from Cassie's face. "Five hundred famous people?"

"Not all super famous," Vanessa waved her concerns away and dug into her purse coming up with a card. She scribbled on the back of it and handed it to Cassie. "Scarlett wants cupcakes at her party."

"Oh. My. God." Tesha grabbed the card. "Scarlett Johansson?"

"Yep," Vanessa clip-clopped toward the door. "See you there." She blew a kiss in his direction and disappeared out the door.

"Aren't you going to see your girlfriend off?" Cassie finally spoke to him. It was on the tip of his tongue to say they weren't an item, but Mark cleared his throat.

Letting out a breath, Jensen stood and went straight through the door and outside without looking at Cassie. "Vanessa, wait up."

His costar's hair swung in perfect synchronicity and fell into place as she strolled to her rental. For a moment, he just stared at it. How did she do that? "What's up with the cupcake hook up?"

"Oh, that." She waved it off. "I love her cakes, she's pretty talented, so why not?"

"I don't think it's a good idea." He inched closer when she frowned. "I know you're trying to do a good thing but think about it. How will she fit in there? The well-known cupcake people in LA won't be happy, they may go after her."

Nothing he said made any sense, of course, but he knew Vanessa would pretend to understand.

"You know, you're right. I'll text Cassie and tell her Scarlett changed her mind." She pulled out her cell.

"Yes, she's not the LA type."

"I wouldn't tell Cassie that."

"Tell me what?" Cassie stood behind him. Her voice was an octave higher than normal.

"Oh, there you are," Vanessa said and pulled Jensen to her side. "I don't think they will need you in LA after all."

Cassie's gaze traveled slowly from Vanessa to him. Hurt mixed with anger shone in her wide eyes.

"I appreciate the thought, Vanessa. But Jensen is right. I am not the type. I would never fit in your world." She spun on her heel, and with her head held high, went back to the house.

"Oh, boy. Her best friend is marrying your brother. I'd watch my back around her if I were you." Vanessa kissed his cheek and trotted to her car.

Hands jammed into his pants pockets, he stared at the ground. When it came to Cassie, he was extra adept at messing things up. He'd meant to protect her from what was sure to be a cancellation, but instead now Cassie probably thought he was being an asshole again. He knew Vanessa would forget to tell Scarlett and when Cassie called, the actress would probably string her along, even going as far as a week prior before canceling, if she did at all.

He went to Tesha's house and looked around. "If you're looking for Cassie, she just went in my office. What did you do this time, Jensen?" Tesha blocked his way, hands on her hips. "Why don't you just stop? If you don't like her, then stay away from her."

"I didn't mean to hurt her feelings. I was trying…let me talk to her."

With a roll of her eyes, she stepped aside and motioned for him to pass. Cassie stood at the window, she looked out and didn't turn when he walked in. "Please just go away. Leave me alone."

"You don't understand."

Cassie swung to face him, her face scrunched up in anger as she stalked to him. "I understand perfectly. I'm not good enough to fit into the elite LA society. I would embarrass you if I dared to say I knew you."

She wiped an errant tear with the back of her hand. "Maybe you're right. I don't know anything about being rich. But I know that I'd be okay if you never spoke to me again."

"I'm sorry."

She didn't reply, instead brushed past him back to the kitchen and began cleaning up.

His phone rang. It was his mother.

"Jensen?" His mother's voice was unsteady. "You have to come home now. Bring Tesha."

"Is it Adam?"

"No, Caden. He's been shot. They aren't sure he'll make it. Hurry, honey." He heard her sniff.

"I'll be there in an hour."

"Please, honey, drive carefully, and don't speed. I don't want to worry about something happening to you."

"Yes Ma'am. I love you."

"I love you, too, baby."

He took off at a run. "Tesha!"

AT TESHA'S INSISTENCE, Cassie came along. She sat in the back seat of Adam's black '68 Ford Fairlane. Jensen drove fast, but did not go past the speed limit by much. The quiet tension in the vehicle was tangible.

No matter how angry she was at Jensen, at the moment she wanted to be there for Tesha and Adam. The entire way, Tesha spoke on the phone with Adam or Miriam Ford, Jensen's mother, and gave them updates.

Caden had been taken in for emergency surgery. He'd been shot four times. Two bullets penetrated his bulletproof vest and struck him in the abdomen. The other two shots hit his upper arm and left thigh.

Finally, they turned down Broadway in Nashville toward Vanderbilt University Hospital. Cassie let out a breath as they slowed down. "Pull up to the entrance. Both of you go inside. I'll park and find you."

Neither argued.

She watched Jensen take Tesha's hand and lead her inside. A part of her ached at seeing the closeness brought by times like this. Tesha had found a new family with the Fords. Maybe one day she'd be lucky enough to meet someone who would treasure her and bring her into the family like Adam had Tesha.

After parking, she made her way to the ER entrance, her gaze fixed straight ahead, while praying that Caden would be all right. Just as she entered through the sliding doors, Tristan Ford caught up with her. The usually stoic man's face was even more so, his expression carved from stone. Without speaking, he took her arm, and they walked together to a waiting room where the rest of the family was huddled.

Miriam Ford was ensconced in Jensen's arms, her face hidden into his shoulder. Tesha leaned on Adam's shoulder who sat in a chair looking blankly toward a wall. The patriarch of the family, Roman, stood by watching over his family with a pained expression.

They looked up as she and Tristan neared. No one said anything. Jensen's gaze flickered to where Tristan held her arm, but then he returned his attention to their mother.

Rows of uncomfortable chairs filled the overly air-conditioned room. On each beige wall one large abstract painting was centered. Cassie absently wondered who picked the ugly art for hospitals. Anyone with half a brain would know scenic pictures of open land with horses or some sort of ranch scene would be better suited that the ridiculous splatters of paint. The window were thick glass panes that didn't open. Lord forbid anyone let in some fresh air.

In the background phones rang and elevators dinged, the only noises besides the occasional comment from one member of the family to another.

An hour later a doctor finally appeared, and everyone except Adam, who remained as if in a trance, jumped to their feet.

The doctor looked to Roman, who stood the closest, his arm protectively around his wife.

"Caden has made it through the surgery. He lost a lot of blood, and we had to remove one of his kidneys. But the other kidney is healthy. I am cautiously optimistic. The next few hours will tell."

"When can I see him, Patrick?" Miriam touched the doctor's forearm.

Cassie realized the resemblance between the physician and the Fords. Same dark hair and blue eyes, same stature, with wide shoulders. She glanced at the doctor's nametag. Patrick Ford. Ah, a relative.

Dr. Ford smiled at Jensen's mother. "I promise I'll get you back to see him as soon as possible, Aunt Miriam. He's in recovery right now." The doctor left after promising to return as soon as he had news.

Cassie sat next to Tesha, who held Adam's hand. Her friend let out a breath. "I appreciate you being here."

"Don't thank me. That's what friends do."

Jensen paced the length of a wall on his cell phone, while explaining to his manager why he couldn't be there. By his end of the conversation, they seemed to be demanding he return immediately. The world he chose to live in had no compassion, no care for family or any life other than what revolved around them. How could someone who came from such a strong, close-knit family choose to live in that world?

Cassie's attention was taken from Jensen when Tesha got to her feet and stood in front of Adam. "Adam, look at me."

It was then that Cassie noticed Adam was gripping the arms of the chair, his arms trembling and face ashen. He suffered from extreme PTSD, an after effect of three deployments to Afghanistan. It was understandable that his youngest brother being shot would catapult him into an episode.

Jensen must have also seen it because he moved Tesha aside. He kneeled before his brother and gave him a cocky grin.

"Hey, Adam. I have something to tell you. Don't yell until I finish and don't deck me, cause I need my face to stay pretty for an interview tomorrow." He waited a beat and finally Adam's gaze moved to him.

"What?"

"I drove the Fairlane here."

Adam's eyes widened.

Although Jensen acted as if he didn't notice, Cassie knew he did. "It ran like a champ, but I think it needs a few tweaks. I heard a small knocking noise. I'll work on it this week. Get under the hood and tighten up a few things."

"Don't touch my car," Adam growled; his body lost some of its tension, but his gaze remained glazed over.

"What? Don't you don't trust me? I'm a great driver, unlike the rest of you. I'll just pop the hood and take a look. Let you know what I think is wrong. How about that?"

Finally Adam looked to his brother's face. "Did you really hear something or are you just B.S.ing me? What do you think is wrong?"

Jensen began rattling off what he thought should be done to the car and engaged his brother into the conversation of what they could do to the car, which once belonged to Adam's best friend. The friend who'd died in Afghanistan.

It never ceased to amaze Cassie how Jensen managed to switch personalities so easily, from total jerk to nice guy. She dragged her gaze away wishing to be anywhere but in the same room with Jensen Ford. Tesha leaned against her and took her hand. "You're probably ready to get some sleep."

Both looked to the large clock on the wall. It was almost midnight. "I am a bit tired, but I want to wait until you get news. I couldn't possibly sleep right now."

As if summoned by her words the doctor appeared again. "Uncle Roman and Aunt Miriam, come with me. Caden is awake." Patrick Ford looked past the older couple to everyone else. "He's still not out of the woods, but the fact he's coherent and asked to see his mom and dad, is a good sign."

Tristan went to the door and spoke to the doctor while Jensen and Adam hovered, surrounding their cousin.

The sun had risen by the time everyone had been in to see

Caden. After everyone had witnessed with their own eyes that he was alive, it seemed the tension somewhat dissipated.

"Tesha, why don't you and Cassie go to the house and rest for a bit?" Mrs. Ford looked to her sons. "I doubt I can get any of these knuckleheads to leave so I won't ask. But one of you take the girls home to get some sleep."

The three men looked at each other as if by some sort of telepathy the driver would appear. Finally Jensen huffed. "Fine, I'll take them."

Cassie shook her head. "I can drive. I had a short nap a bit ago. You stay here."

Tesha hugged her soon to be mother-in-law. "Please call me if anything comes up. I will be back in a few hours."

In the car, Tesha let out a breath. "I can't stand it. Just when things are good, something always seems to happen. Adam has been doing great the last few weeks. This could set him back a bunch." She let out a sniff. "Caden has to be okay. I'm not sure I can stand the idea of life without the little brother."

"Little?" Cassie snorted. "He's a six-foot-four tall hunk. Hard to think of him as the 'little' one." She smiled at Tesha. "He'll be fine. The doctor said he was doing good."

Tesha let out a breath. "Yes, he did, didn't he?"

"We're not going to get any sleep, are we?"

"Nope."

They pulled into the Waffle House parking lot, and both stared at the huge yellow letters on the side of the building. "You are the best friend ever." Tesha grinned. "There's nothing to reassure a person like hash browns and a big waffle."

Arms linked, they walked into to the restaurant and were immediately overcome by the mixture of wonderful aromas and cheerful hellos.

Chapter Twelve

"Yᴏᴜ ʟᴏᴏᴋ ʟɪᴋᴇ shit." Jensen was instantly awake at his brother's statement. He'd snuck into Caden's room and promptly camped out on the empty bed next to his.

"Yeah, well, you're not exactly lookin' GQ cover ready." He yawned so wide his jaw popped. "What the hell are you doing awake? It's like…" By the brightness of the sun, it was about midday. "…noon or something," he finished.

The blood pressure machine beeped, and both looked at it. "What the hell?" Caden pushed a button, and it went silent.

The cocky bastard had the nerve to chuckle. "You slept through Mom and Dad coming in to tell me they were going home to get some rest. Adam is somewhere rattling around the hallways. Said he was getting coffee. Refuses to leave."

Jensen swung his legs down to the floor. "Shit, I need to go look for him."

"Nah, he's fine." Caden groaned and his face constricted. He glared at the ceiling. "What you need to do is get me out of here."

"Are you fucking kidding me?" Jensen gave his brother an incredulous look. "A few hours ago they didn't know if we were going shopping for a long ass coffin, and you think I'm helping you get up and go? Hell, no. You, little bro, are staying here until Patrick says you can leave."

"I am not about to lay in a stupid coffin, hair all gooped up and plastered on top of my head. If I croak, promise me you'll set me on fire."

"Wanna practice now?" Jensen couldn't help but laugh. His brother was going to recover. Everything would be all right in his world. "Shit. Where's my phone?"

"Adam took it. It wouldn't stop buzzing and it was bothering the patient." Caden grinned. "I'm not to be bothered, apparently."

"Ugh!" Jensen fell back into the bed. "They must be shitting bricks right now. The film is already behind. Couldn't you have waited a week to get shot?"

"Sorry. Next time I'll have the gunman check your schedule." Caden slurred and his eyelids drooped; Jensen watched as his brother's face went slack as he fell asleep and let out even breaths. Jensen reached and touched his brother's shoulder, needing the reassurance.

"Hey." Patrick walked in, looked at Caden, and then checked the chart.

"Is he going to be all right?"

His cousin nodded and let out a breath. "Yeah. He looks good. Barring an infection, I'm optimistic he'll be arguing to get released in a couple days."

"Try a couple hours. He already asked me to break him out."

"That's why we give him sleepy meds." Patrick studied Jensen. "How are things with you? The movie business seems to be treating you well."

"Yeah. It's good." He looked to the window. "Great."

"That bad, huh?" Patrick let out a breath. "It's okay to step back. Take a break. You've been going at it pretty hard for the last few years. Take some Jensen time."

As if the thought had not occurred to him. "I'm an idiot. Signed a contract for another movie in a couple months. So there goes another six months of my life."

"After that?"

"Releases. Carpets to walk, interviews to do and Oscars to accept. You know, the usual."

"Oscars? Really?" Patrick lifted an eyebrow, his green eyes accessing him. "That would be cool. But you'll have to make one of those boring movies only critics watch."

"Damn, I knew I was doing something wrong."

Once Patrick left, promising to come back to see Caden in a few hours, except for the bleeps of the machines around Caden's bed, the room was peaceful. It had been a long time since he'd been able to just lay around with only his thoughts for company. The ability to think without a phone call or person demanding his attention was something he rarely experienced.

From the window, Jensen watched people hurry to their cars to avoid the rain, and a mother laughing when her toddler lifted her face and opened her mouth to catch raindrops.

In between the filming he'd do more of this. Stay at Adam's house and chill, take time to consider what to do after the next movie. Maybe it was time to do what Patrick suggested.

Step away for a bit.

"THAT'S A WRAP!" A week later the director called out and put a hand on Jensen's shoulder squeezing it. "We'll be done in a couple days. Good thing you decided to put in the extra time."

The people mulled about; most had nothing much to do and were anxious to leave Lovely.

The novelty of the small town had worn off weeks ago and they were ready to head back to the city, traffic, and hurried life.

Once he grabbed his jacket and sunglasses, Jensen decided to take a drive into town for dinner. He'd become addicted to the diner's shepherd's pie.

About a mile from town he saw a familiar figure walking on the side of the road. He pulled over and got out of the car. "Cassie, you okay?"

"Heading to town. My car broke down a mile back."

He'd been so focused on dinner, he'd not noticed. "What's wrong with it?"

It was surprising to see how non-pulsed she was by the situation. Her lips curved. "It's a piece of shit. Old and needs to take regular naps."

"Come on, I'll drive you to town. Then I'll come back and take a look at it."

Once settled into the passenger seat, she let out a breath. "Seems you're always driving me around. What will I do when you leave? No one to drive and piss me off."

"I can call and annoy you." He grinned at her. "Wanna eat with me? I don't feel like eating alone."

"Sure." Her answer surprised him, and he let out a breath he wasn't aware he'd been holding. "But I'll need a ride home after. Not in the mood to swim."

The steady rainfall had turned into thunder and heavy

downpour. "You got a deal."

The diner was not very busy, due to the bad weather. Just a few patrons lingered at the four-seat tables. The aroma of garlic and other delights made his stomach grumble, and Jensen made a beeline for a booth.

He couldn't help but note she kept studying him while they ate and talked. Finally he had to ask. "Why do you keep staring at me?"

Her pretty eyes narrowed at him. "This is about the time when you're going to turn into an asshole. We've been getting along too well for the last hour."

"Nah. I'm an asshole all the time, you just haven't noticed that I've been spitting into your plate."

Her bark of laughter made the people at the other tables turn to them. Most had become used to his presence, but he noticed a pair of women attempting to hide the fact they were taking his picture with their cell phones by pretending to take pictures of each other. If somehow the pictures made it to a gossip magazine, Mark would have a cow.

He lifted his hand to the side of his face and peeked through his fingers. The women were older, late fifties he guessed. They were giggling behind their hands and whispering.

Cute.

"The food here is incredible," Jensen told Cassie. He didn't want to go just yet. Didn't want to leave the diner and drop her off.

She drank her sweet tea, and their eyes met over the rim of the glass. "I'm glad my car broke down. This has been nice." She shocked him by covering his hand with hers. "Thank you for helping me out. Let me pay for dinner."

"Are you going to expect me to put out?" He smiled at her pretty blush. "Because I'm not that kind of guy."

"Whatever." She slapped his shoulder and picked up the ticket. "Come on, I have to hurry home. My plant is lonely."

Once in the car, Jensen drove below the speed limit. "What about your brother, isn't he there?"

"No, he's gone to college. He'll be home on the weekends he doesn't work." She fumbled in her purse for her keys. "Would you mind pulling into the driveway? It's a doozy out there."

He pulled in and there was an awkward moment. Both looked forward. Finally he turned to her. "Can I come in?"

They were soaked by the time they made it inside the doorway. He didn't wait for her to say anything, but took her mouth instantly, tasting sweet tea and promise. She moaned and wrapped her arms around his neck, her fingers raking through his hair.

No words were needed, both knew it was best not to speak. She yanked at his clothing while kicking off her shoes and he did the same. Both unbuttoned, unzipped and tore clothes away, leaving a path of clothing to the bedroom.

In her bra and panties, she was the most beautiful sight, but Jensen didn't have the patience to look right now; the need to touch her was too great, so he pulled her against him. Her skin was cool to the touch, and she shivered when he ran his hands up and down her back.

Cassie lifted her face, and he took her mouth once again while walking her backwards to the bed. They slid between the blankets and snuggled against each other.

Her curves were a novelty, a rare find. He never thought to have a chance with her, to feel her plush body against his. When she ran her hands up his chest he let out a low groan and rolled Cassie onto her back. Laying over her, it was hard not to speed things up, but he forced himself to go slow. He wanted to make this memorable, ensure each moment was prolonged, never let her go.

He reached around and unfastened her bra and slid it away. Her generous breasts fell free, and he took to them. Suckling at one while fondling the other, he paid attention to each one, his tongue flicking over the hardening tips while he circled her other nipple with the pad of his finger.

"Oh." Cassie was overwhelmed by sensations. She ran her nails down Jensen's back until reaching the curve of his taut butt. The man was built perfectly, his amazing body matching the gorgeous face. She refused to consider anything other than enjoying the present.

And oh boy, was the present amazing. Jensen lifted from her breasts, his lips swollen from her kisses, and smiled at her. She opened her mouth to say something, but his hand slid between her legs and speech evaded her. "Ah." Her eyes rolled back when he slid his finger through her center and one into her sex.

The man definitely knew what he was doing. He licked his way down the center of her body to swirl his tongue into her belly button while his hand did delightful things between her legs. Her hips lifted into his hand, urging him to continue.

"Come for me, Cassie." His darkened gaze met hers. She closed her eyes and pushed her head against the pillow when the heat spread up her body. When his hot mouth took her breasts again, she was lost. The combination of sensations sent her to lose control, and she cried out.

Jensen continued to caress her until she was on the brink again.

"My turn." She pushed at his shoulders and rolled him to his back. It was time to do some exploring. After all, it was doubtful she'd ever have the chance to again.

She climbed over him and straddled his slender hips. Unable to keep from running her gaze down his wonderful body, taking in the sight of his muscular, yet slender physique, Cassie ran her hands down his broad chest, enjoying the feel of rippling muscles. She then leaned forward and ran her tongue down and across his tight abs, while teasing the tight nipples with her fingers. She moved her palms down his sides while her mouth traveled to between his legs. His sex was hard, needing attention. She took him in hand while tracing the tip of her tongue around the tip.

By the deep grunts he made, Jensen was in a happy place. Cassie took him into her mouth and proceeded to take all he had to give.

"I don't want to come yet." He pulled her up and drove his tongue into her mouth.

His large hand circled her waist, and he lifted her so that he could drive into her.

Cassie's only thought was. "Oh, yeah."

"CASSIE?" THE DEEP voice penetrated through the fogginess

and Cassie wished it away. She didn't want to wake up from the delightful dream. It felt so real still. As if encased in strong arms, held against a hard body. In her dream it had been the perfect way to fall asleep after several bouts of lovemaking.

Now whoever it was tried to drag her away from the best sex dream ever. Her and...

"Holy shit!" She bolted upright and heard a muffled curse. Jensen lay next to her, with a hand on his jaw.

"You just elbowed the crap out of me."

"What?....What? Did we? Oh..." She fell back onto the bed and squeezed her eyes shut. What had she done?

"Don't you have to be at Tesha's to make breakfast?" He tapped her shoulder. When she didn't reply, he kissed it. "I'm hungry."

Against her hip she felt something and immediately her stupid body went into slut-mode.

An hour later, both were showered and dressed. She slugged into the kitchen to find a fresh cup of coffee and one of her cupcakes on a plate. At her kitchen table, Jensen stretched and presented her with a wide grin.

"Ready? I have to be on set in fifteen."

So they weren't going to talk about it. Too overwhelmed to consider that she'd slept with someone who was dating another woman and who was a mega star.

Right. She decided it was best not to think. "Yep, let's go."

It would have been easy to pretend they'd not slept together if not for the trail of her clothes that remained on the floor. "Shit." She kicked her still wet jeans aside and picked up her raincoat.

"I think I'm mad at myself. Let's not talk."

"Oh, we're gonna talk." Jensen grinned at her.

"No, we are not."

An hour later, when her cup of coffee hit the floor and the hot liquid splashed onto her legs, Cassie let out a curse and jumped away. One of the ladies, Donna, gave her a curious look. "Are you all right?"

No, she wasn't. Why had she not thought about it until just then? She and Jensen had not used any protection. She wasn't on birth control. There hadn't been any reason to be. He was a famous person, for lord's sake, one would think the idiot would make sure not to get someone pregnant.

Cassie let out a breath and looked through the windows toward the house next door. Maybe he'd had a vasectomy and didn't worry about it. But then again, the dumbass should worry about STDs.

"Oh my God!" She covered her face with her hands. What if she caught something from him?

"Honey, did you burn yourself? What's wrong?" The woman took her arm and guided her to a chair. "Sit down, I'll get you a glass of water."

"No, thank you Debbie." She jumped to her feet. "I have to go next door. I'll be back in a bit."

Chapter Thirteen

"Son of a bitch!" Jensen stared wide-eyed at the display on the screen, not seeing a thing.

The actor next to him pushed him aside and studied the picture. "What?"

"Nothing. I need a grab some water." He went to the food table, his head spinning. He'd not used protection the night before. Although he felt confident Cassie did not sleep around, he hoped she was on birth control.

What was the matter with him? Jensen gulped the entire bottle down and felt better. Of course she was on birth control, she'd not allowed him to do…so many things. He let out a breath to keep from getting aroused again.

"Jensen?" her voice sent a ping straight to his crotch and Mr. Happy sprung to life. "I need to ask you something."

Cassie's round eyes met his.

"What did I do now?"

She grabbed his arm and dragged him away from the people who watched them with interest. "Please tell me you've been neutered."

His stomach sank and somehow spit caught in his throat and he began to cough. "I'm not a dog."

"Ssshhh!" she pulled him a few feet further away from the set. "Last night. We didn't use a condom." She swallowed and looked past him to the people behind him. "I'm not on the pill."

Nothing occurred to him. His mind went blank, and he froze. This was her way of getting back at him for the cupcake thing. Any moment now she'd laugh and tell him it was a joke. Or maybe she'd drag it out for a day or two.

He relaxed and shrugged. "I hope you're joking cause I'm sure I've got some strong swimmers." He grinned and let out a breath. "I gotta get back."

"You don't understand." Her fingers dug into his arm. "I. Am. Not. On. The. Pill."

If she was joking, he had to give it to her. She was a good actress because she still looked panicked.

"I. Have. To. Get. Back," he replied, speaking as slowly as she had. "Stop. Joking."

"Oh my God." She hit his shoulder. "Will you please be serious?"

"Are you being serious?" He studied her face through narrowed eyes. "Cause I can't act if I'm passed out."

"I am serious, Jensen. Look, I just need you to tell me I shouldn't worry about it. Please." She looked up at him, and he couldn't help the urge to hold the woman and reassure her. Unfortunately, they had an audience.

"There's nothing to worry about." He gave her his best nonchalant look. "I'm not."

He walked away from her, but his mind stayed behind. What the hell had he done? At the thought of Cassie pregnant with his child, a smile tugged at his lips, and he had to shake his head. He'd totally lost his mind.

His cell rang. It was Caden. "Come get me out of here. I'm

leaving with or without your help. Tristan and Adam already said no."

"Yeah, okay. But I can't be there until this evening. Can you wait until then?" Jensen replied and hung up after Caden agreed to wait.

He called his mother next, and she was already on her way to the hospital. She'd put a stop to Caden's plan. If his brother resisted, she'd go to Patrick about it.

Chachi, the make up artist, rushed towards him, a big pink brush in his hand. "We have to get you done. Come on, you're all shiny and shit."

He allowed the man to pull him toward the make up trailer. "Hey Chachi, how long does it take for a woman to know if she's pregnant?"

"How the fuck should I know?" Chachi gave an exaggerated shudder. "My cousin Marisol said she knows like within hours. But that bitch is always pregnant, so she's probably just making it up."

"Hours?" Jensen tried to look out the window, but Chachi held his head still and began to do whatever he did to his hair.

The wardrobe woman came in and plopped onto a chair, she texted while frowning. "Damn teenagers. They should all be sent off to live on an island until they are twenty-five."

Chachi laughed. "Hey, we have a question. How long does it take for a woman to find out she's knocked up?" The stylist held a comb in the air waiting for a reply.

The woman stared at Chachi with her mouth open. "You had sex with a woman?"

Fortunately Chachi was smart enough to know Jensen would kill him if he divulged it was him who wanted to know.

"Ewww. Hell no. I was just telling Jensen here that my cousin Marisol claims that she can tell within hours."

"Oh." The woman stared at her phone. "There are tests that tell within like a day, but it could be weeks." She let out a breath and stared at her phone. "China has a good plan. No more than one child per family. Kids suck."

She jumped up. "Gotta scoot." The door slammed after her and Jensen stared at Chachi in the mirror. "I think kids are cool."

Chachi shuddered. "I don't like how they are so little and shit."

He didn't see Cassie the rest of the day. Once they finished shooting for the day, he rushed to his bike and sped to her house. The windows were dark, and no one answered when he knocked. A dog barked in the distance and an old lady peered at him through her screen door. "Cassie's probably at the cupcake shop."

"Thanks," Jensen called out and went back to his bike and headed the two miles to town. Once there he parked in front of the cupcake shop. When he tried the door it was locked. There was a hastily written sign taped to the inside.

"Closed due to illness."

Had she gotten sick because she was pregnant? He pulled out his phone and Googled the question. He got a bunch of confusing links that didn't make any sense. Next he called Tesha.

"Do you know where Cassie is?" He asked without preamble. "I need to talk to her. I think she's sick."

"Sick?" Tesha replied and said something to someone else.

Probably Adam.

"I'll call her. I would give you her number, but she'll probably kill me. You two are always at odds."

"We were not at odds last night," he blurted and then hoped she'd not ask any questions.

Tesha humphed. "You ruined her chance to cater for Scarlett Johansson."

"Oh yeah, well…"

"So I will call and ensure she is okay and call you back." He stared at the phone when she hung up, not sure what to do next.

A couple came up and looked from the door to him. The woman, who looked to be in her sixties, asked to take a picture with him and her husband, took it with an iPad. She looked at the note on the door. "I hope Cassie is okay. Or maybe someone in her family is sick."

"Its too bad. I really wanted cupcake and some coffee," her husband grumbled as they walked away. Some teenagers ambled by and stopped at the door; unaware of who he was, they left while one talked on the phone to whoever was to meet them there.

Mrs. Miller, the owner of the hardware store, waved him over, and he jogged across the street. "Hey there, sweetie. I have a key to the shop if you need to pick up some cupcakes."

"Uh…no, I was actually looking for Cassie." He watched as she rounded the counter and climbed up on her stool. Almost at eye level, she smiled at him. "She had to go to Nashville. Take care of something. I think she was headed to a hospital or clinic or something."

His eyes widened. Was Cassie getting some sort of morning after treatment? "Can you try to remember which one? Did she look sick?"

Mrs. Miller frowned. "No, she seemed fine. Is something wrong with someone in your family? Is it Adam?"

Everyone in town knew Adam since he'd lived there up until a few weeks earlier, when he'd gone back to Nashville to work for Ford Industries. "Adam is fine. Thanks. I'll see you later, Mrs. Miller."

"Let me know who's sick," she called after him.

If he had to go to every clinic and hospital in Nashville, he was going to do anything in his power to stop her. How could she do whatever it was women did without talking to him first? Damn woman didn't even give him a chance to tell her he loved her.

The realization stopped him dead in his tracks. Jensen stood in the middle of the street until a slow-moving truck honked and forced him into action.

"What the hell am I thinking?" He raked his fingers through his hair and let out a breath.

"No. No. No." He paced in front of the cupcake shop too shaken to get on his motorcycle. "Big mistake. Or not. Maybe it's a good thing. She hates me. But she slept with me. Shit."

"Mind your language, young man." An elderly woman tugged at the cupcake shop's door oblivious to the sign.

"It's closed, ma'am. Excuse my language."

She peered up at him and lifted her cane to point at him. "Your mother will hear about this, Adam Ford." Her cane lowered, she shuffled away.

His phone finally rang. Tesha returned his call. "So, what's going on."

"Nothing really." Tesha was quiet. "She's visiting a friend who's in the hospital."

"Are you sure she's not the one who's sick?"

"Yes. What is up with you?" Tesha sounded worried. "Did you do something to her? What have you done this time?"

"Nothing. Well, not anything. I just need to talk to her."

"Jensen. I can only ask you to hold off until she gets back. She's dealing with something delicate right now. Two trips to the same hospital can get a person down. She doesn't need you making her upset again."

They hung up and Jensen mounted his bike. He'd get his jag and then go to Nashville.

Once there, he'd get her to leave the hospital and assure her. He would be a good father. Hopefully she would believe him when he told her how he felt.

Luckily, an hour later, he was able to get a close parking spot. Jensen pulled his baseball cap low over his face and walked past the reception area to the elevators. Once inside, he pushed the fourth-floor button. Thanks to Google he found out that was the women's delivery floor. The elevator stopped at the third and he caught sight of Cassie walking into a room. He shoved his arm to the closing door and got out.

"Can I help you, sir?" A nurse eyed him as if trying to place him. "Which patient are you here to see?"

"Miss Tucker," he replied looking to the doorway where Cassie had gone into. "She's right there." He pointed and turned away while the nurse watched him.

The door was slightly opened, and he pushed it wider. There was a drawn curtain so she could not see him.

"I didn't think you'd come. Didn't think you believed me."

A male voice sounded. "I hoped you would."

"Its a lot to take in," Cassie replied to whoever it was.

"Did you consider my proposal?"

"Yes."

Jensen jumped when a nurse tapped him on the shoulder. "Sir, this is not the right room."

"Yes, it is." He replied. "I just saw her."

Cassie appeared and pushed him out of the room, closing the door behind them. "What are you doing here?"

"I came to stop you from doing something stupid."

"What?" She pulled him further away to stand in front of the elevators. "You followed me here?" At her incredulous look, he wasn't sure what to say.

"You were upset about not using protection. Then you put a sign on the shop door. I figured you were doing something rash."

"Like?" She crossed her arms and frowned.

"Who's the guy?" He changed tactic. Before he'd spilled his guts, it was best to have all the facts.

"You are confusing me. It's none of your business why I'm here."

And of course his stupid temper snapped like a twig under Big Foot's...foot. "What the fuck is it with you? I asked you a question, woman. Why can't you just answer me?"

She looked down the hallway towards the room she'd just vacated and then back to him. "The man in the room is my ex-fiancé. We are getting back together." Cassie pointed to the elevator. "Please leave."

"What if you're pregnant from last night?" He didn't budge. "What then?"

"Its nothing I can't handle."

"You're not getting an abortion."

Cassie stared at him agog. "I can't believe we're having this conversation. I'm in a damn hospital. You have done nothing but make my life miserable since I met you. You insult me, ruined my chance to cater to Scarlett Fucking Johansson's party. You are a pompous asshole. Yes, last night happened. It was good, but a huge mistake."

She lowered her voice to a hiss. "Jensen, you are the last person I want to be tied to for the rest of my life. So, I'll get a morning after pill, or pack or whatever the hell it is, and take it. Because Jensen Ford, I would rather overdose than have your child." She turned and stalked back to the room.

"Who is he?" the nurse asked obviously overhearing part of their conversation.

"The biggest asshole known to mankind," Cassie said and went into the room.

The elevator doors slid open, beckoning to take him away from the strange pain in his chest.

He stalked into his brother's room, his head pounding. Caden opened his eyes and blinked. "What happened to you?"

"I'm pissed. So damn mad right now." Jensen walked across the room and peered down at his brother. "Am I an asshole?"

"Sorta," Caden pushed a button, and the bed lifted him to sit. "Why?"

"I'm being serious." Why was everyone being such a pain in the ass today?

"All right. Tell me what happened."

"This woman, she just said she'd rather overdose than

spend her life with me."

Caden's eyes bugged. "Holy shit. Did you just ask someone to marry you, and they turned you down like that." He slapped his thigh and winced. "Ow!" Caden grinned. "That is one thing I would never see happening."

"I didn't ask her to marry me." Jensen noticed his brother looked better, his coloring normal.

Decided to stop being self-centered for a few. "You're still here. That's good."

"Yeah. Mom threatened me." Caden grinned. "So you've fallen in love, huh? I'm so glad it's you and not me. Love sucks."

"Answer my question, Bro." Jensen noticed Caden seem to struggle for an answer.

"You are really giving. Very nice to the family. And you seem to be nice to your coworkers. They love you. But when it comes to women, from what I see you keep them at arm's distance. I've never seen you in love, but I bet you throw up all kinds of smoke grenades to keep them from seeing the real you."

Caden shrugged. "Sorry this lady hurt your feelings. I'm sure she'll come around."

ONCE IN THE hospital parking lot, Jensen leaned on his car and pondered what Caden had said. Perhaps it was true.

His phone vibrated; it was Mark, his agent. "I have you set up for three interviews next week in New York. Flying out first thing in the morning."

He kicked at his car tire. "What part of I'm taking a couple weeks off did you not understand?"

"Did you read my texts?"

"No, I was at the hospital…visiting my brother."

"Why didn't you tell me you and the cupcake girl were messing around? Someone released a video of you two making out at her shop. You have to fix it. They're saying you cheated on Vanessa."

"How bad is it?" He hurried to get into the car to see if he could bring up the video.

"Let's just say Cassie Tucker's friends will be high-fiving her. It's pretty steamy."

Jensen hung up while Mark was speaking. He stared into the distance and considered how far he could get before he ran out of gas. Stop in some cheap pay by the night motel, hide for several weeks.

If Cassie hated him now, when she found out about the video, it would crush her. Not to mention it could hurt her business. Small town people had long memories.

He'd be on the plane in the morning. Whatever happened, he'd ensure Cassie was kept from harm.

"Welcome Jensen Ford, ladies and gentlemen," the talk show host stood and shook his hand. Stephen Colbert was one of his favorite hosts, and he'd called in advance to ask his help with the video. This was not one that Mark had set up, so he figured his phone would be ringing off the hook at the impromptu interview once The Late Show aired.

"So everyone's talking about the steamy video of you and a woman named Cassie making out at her cupcake shop. What was that all about? Someone new in your life?"

Jensen winked at the camera and grinned. "I save a lot of money that way, it's how I pay for food." The audience barked with laughter.

He waited until they quieted. "Seriously. It was supposed to be a private moment between a beautiful woman and me. Our first kiss. It was great." The audience gave a collective "Awww."

"What about Vanessa? This kiss happened just prior to you going to Cabo with her."

Jensen let out a sigh and looked down. "The trip to Cabo was prearranged by our agents. It was purely platonic. We're just good friends."

A picture popped up on the screen behind him of him and Vanessa kissing in the water. "What about these shots?" Stephen asked, his expression curious. "Looks like more than just friends." He held up finger quotes.

"We were playing to the paparazzi." Jensen pointed at the screen. "I lost those sunglasses. Those are my favorite sunglasses. If someone finds them, mail them to me, please." The audience laughed again, and he waited for the next question.

The talk show host looked to the screen where a picture of him and Cassie was splashed. They were kissing, her arms around his neck, and her legs circling his waist. He held her up on the counter, his fingers in her hair. The audience's "oohs" and "oh wow's," echoed what he wanted to say out loud.

"How are things now between you and Miss Tucker?"

He smiled toward the audience. "I wish I could say it's a

happy ending. Right now she's not speaking to me. I was hopeful she'll give me a chance, but I supposed she won't give me the time of day once she finds out about the video."

"I find it hard to believe American's Sexiest Man Alive can't get his girl. We'll be rooting for you." Stephen said and the audience burst into applause.

Thankfully the airport as one of the few places he had an easy time blending into the crowd. With a duffle bag in hand, baseball cap and scuffed up boots, he lowered to a chair and awaited his flight. A news clip caught his attention it was his interview at the Late Show, under it the caption *Sexiest Man Alive admits to being unlucky in love*.

On the drive back to Lovely from the Nashville airport, the phone finally stopped vibrating.

Jensen knew Mark was livid and decided not to answer when the man would be screaming into his ear. He waited for the call to go to message and then called Adam.

"Hey Bro, don't sell the house in Lovely to anyone. I'll buy it. Need a place to get away. It's perfect."

Adam was silent for a few moments. "I'm not selling it. Just use it when you want. It's already paid for. Will that work?"

Yes, it would work. He texted Mark next.

Taking the next couple months off. Put off the next movie or they can get another leading man. Need to work on getting a life. And NO I won't change my mind.

Chapter Fourteen

AFTER HER ENCOUNTER with Jensen at the hospital, Cassie had walked into Nick's room and stood just inside the door. It was hard to not turn around and bolt. Get away from her ex and from every man in the planet.

Upon spotting her, there had been hope in Nick's expression. "I still can't believe you're here. Maybe there is a chance for us after all. Although short it may be."

Cassie went to the bedside and placed her fists on her hips.

"You are not dying, Nick. I talked to the nurse. The cancer was caught early, and you are going to recover. How dare you use this illness? This is almost worse than cheating on me." She was so angry, her voice shook.

"I really do love you so much." He reached for her, and she recoiled. How could this be the same man she'd fallen in love with.

"So much so that you didn't take into consideration I have a life separate from you now? I am letting down a friend that is counting on me right now to help with her business. I have my shop to run, that by the way I had to close for half a day to come here. You are a selfish person Nick. I wish you well, I sincerely do. But you and I…" she waved a hand between them, "…is never going to happen again."

His mouth fell open. "You can't leave me now. This is a

horrible time for me."

"Yes, I imagine it is. That's why I called your mom and dad. They are on their way here. I told them you had cancer and left it at that." She picked up her purse and slung it onto her shoulder. "Goodbye, Nick."

Once ensconced in her car, she covered her face with both hands and cried. There were too many things going on at once. The responsibilities kept her from doing what she really wanted to do: put the car in drive and go; keep going until getting as far away as possible.

Raindrops hit her windshield, and she watched them trail down the glass. The weather matched the gloom inside her.

She formulated a plan to not have to face Jensen. Tesha would be back the next day, and she'd ask her and Debbie to take over her duties. It was time to concentrate on her little shop. Her life, separate from Jensen Ford and all the movie crap.

Her car hesitated, but thankfully came to life. Jensen had fixed it for her. Another thing she owed him. The thought angered her. Once she got home, she'd write him a note. Assure him there was no child and write him a check for fixing her car.

Maybe apologize for the harsh things she'd said to him. Not that it bothered him. He enjoyed goading her too much.

THE ENTIRE WAY and once she got home, her phone did not stop ringing. Finally she gave up and answered it when she saw that Tesha had called twice.

"You have to sit down."

"Oh no, what happened?" Cassie's stomach lurched. Could

the day get any worse? "Please just say it. Don't hold back."

"Okay." Tesha began. "There's a video of you and Jensen making out. You know that day he came to the shop. It's gotten into the hands of the media."

"Oh. My. God." Cassie sunk into her couch and looked at the dark television screen. "How bad is it?"

"It's pretty steamy. Damn girl, you didn't tell me he had you up on the counter."

"Eeeeeeeeeeeeeeeeeeh!" Cassie let out a scream. "No. No. No. This can't be happening."

She could hear Tesha making soothing sounds. "I'm sure Jensen will do something to fix it. They are saying he was cheating on Vanessa."

"How can I show my face at the shop tomorrow? Oh my God." The cherry on top of her horrific day. "Earlier I considered driving off into the sunset. I should have listened to my gut instinct."

Tesha laughed. "It will blow over. I'm sure after a couple weeks…"

"No, it won't. The people of Lovely will never forget this." She let out a soft whine. "That man has been nothing but trouble."

They continued talking; Tesha asked about her visit to the hospital to see Nick, and it helped her forget about her situation for only a few moments.

Sure enough, the next morning her shop was busier than ever. Although no one came right out and asked questions, they made comments that made her wince.

"Did you wipe the counter well, dear?" a woman asked while inspecting it.

"I hear she takes special care of certain clients," a man she didn't recognize mumbled under his breath to another one.

Towards the end of the day Deputy Sebastian Castro walked in. She poured him a cup of coffee and waited for whatever he would say.

His hazel eyes lingered on hers. "You plan on letting go of that cup?"

It was then she realized she was gripping the cup and not releasing it. "I'm sorry, stressful day."

"Anything I can help with?"

Bless him; he didn't have a clue about the whole media blow-up. "Not really. Although I think you just made me feel better by being your normal self."

His lips curved. "I can write you a ticket if that makes you even better."

Cassie laughed. "Let's not take it that far."

When he walked out she watched him linger and speak to a woman with a small boy. If only she'd tried to date him when he'd asked. But she'd been too wrapped up in her recent breakup with Nick at the time.

It was a moot point now. Castro was in a happy relationship, and he and Eliza, from the diner, were perfect for each other.

Chapter Fifteen

"JENSEN. I DIDN'T expect to see you today, son," his father said, pulling a second cup from the cupboard. "Your mom's gone to get Caden."

He accepted the cup of coffee and took a swallow. "He finally talked her into getting him out?"

"Nah, Patrick is discharging him today. Between his grumbling and flirting with the nurses, I'm sure they are happy to get rid of him." Roman Ford laughed. "That boy."

As always being home settled him. After a week of rattling around at Adam's house trying to figure out what to do with his time off, he came to the conclusion that it was best to go ahead and do the movie in New Zealand in a couple of months. After that he'd take a couple years off.

His father settled into a chair and studied him. "You ever plan to come home? We miss you around here, son."

"This is where I'm going to settle. I've got another ten years, then I'm going to retire." He began to discuss his plans to build a house there in Nashville with a contractor friend of the family.

"I'm not going to be a lifer. I love acting, but I hate everything that comes with it."

His father listened. "I don't know how you do it. For a long time your mother and I were worried that the lifestyle would change you. I'm glad you're coming back."

"It did change me for a while. I was disconnected and fell into the whole ego thing. But I'm realizing now that it's not worth it. I don't like being that guy. He's not a very nice person."

His father shrugged. "You have to protect yourself. It's understandable, but not at the expense of losing who you really are. Or hurting someone who cares for you."

"Too late for that. I think I just lost the right woman by being a total ass."

They sat silent for a while. His father looked to him. "Don't give up so easily. You may be able to fix it."

There was a ding on his father's phone, and he motioned for him to get up. "Your brother's here. Let's get him inside and settled."

Caden sat at the couch, refusing to lay down. With a blanket over his lap, remote control in hand and bowl of cereal, he leaned back with a wide grin. "Now things are perfect."

"You're an idiot." Jensen looked down at him with a smile. "I can't believe you still live here."

His mom pushed Jensen aside and place a glass of water on a side table along with two pill bottles. "Even if he didn't live here, he would be staying here. He can't get around that well yet."

His brother's crunching noise made Jensen laugh. "Yeah, poor sick baby."

"Don't be jealous," Caden replied with his mouth full, and swallowed. "Hey, did you fix things with your lady friend?"

Jensen held his breath knowing his mother would pounce on the comment. Sure enough, she was beside him in a flash.

"What lady friend? What did you do?"

"Some woman told him he was an a-hole."

"That's not nice." His mother said, pulling him to the opposite couch. "What did you do?"

His brother ignored his glare. "I insulted what she does for a living. I ruined a chance for her to get a catering job in Hollywood, and I assumed she was going to do something stupid. On that one I may have been right. I don't know for sure yet."

"Does this have to do with that embarrassing video?" His mom's gaze pinpointed him. "Because you owe Cassie an apology."

"For kissing her?" The conversation was going in the wrong direction.

Damn Caden.

"You kissed her like that and then jetted off to Cabo with that floozy, Vanessa. Didn't she sleep with Adam, too?"

Oh boy, his mom knew a lot more than he expected. Jensen squirmed and groaned when he noticed his dad standing in the doorway.

"We don't like that floozy," his brother piped up.

"Shut up, Caden."

"Be nice to your brother. He's medicated," their mother said while glaring at him. It was going to get interesting. When his dad sat at the kitchen counter and watched, Jensen realized it was just the beginning.

"Sit down and explain," his mother left no room for arguments.

Chapter Sixteen

"**H**ELLO, CASSIE," MRS. Miller entered the shop and inhaled deeply. "I just love walking in here. Makes me happy."

In the two weeks since the media issue, she'd managed to regain the normalcy of life. Tesha was right, some singer was caught on camera stumbling down a busy New York street drunk and falling into the street butt naked. It sent the Cassie and Jensen episode into yesterday's news.

"How are you today, Mrs. Miller?" She waited for the woman to approach the counter and choose a cupcake.

Instead, Mrs. Miller stared at her. "I desperately need your help. I'm alone at the hardware store and can't get a display moved. It's on rollers but takes two people to maneuver it around. Could you be a doll and run over for just a bit?"

"Oh. Of course." Cassie rounded the corner and pulled her key ring from her apron pocket. "I need some fresh air anyway."

Once inside the hardware store, in the entrance a short shelf on wheels with a display of differing kinds of tools blocked their way. They moved around it, and she picked up on of the tools.

"What a cute hammer." The handles of the tools were decorated in different bright colors patterns.

"Tools for women," Mrs. Miller said, going to the other end. "Now I just need to position this, so it catches the eye when people enter, but doesn't block so much."

Once that was done, Cassie walked out and stood on the sidewalk. Main Street Lovely was quiet, just a few people making their way to the diner. It was three in the afternoon. Too early for the after-work customers, and parents were picking up children from school.

She dug her hands into her apron pockets and looked across the street to her shop. An SUV was parked in front of it. The tan and green paint matched her shop perfectly. Curious, she walked toward it then her eyes rounded. On the side of the car was her shop's logo. *Sweet Indulgence,* in slanted italics, surrounded by the outline of a cupcake.

"Of all the crappy things to do." Cassie walked around the SUV, her hand trailing on its surface.

"That damn Jensen." On the back windshield was an acrylic outline of a woman holding up a cupcake. Cartoony Cassie was cute. "I'm going to kick him in the kneecap for this."

Her mouth fell open when peering into the passenger seat. On it was a single pink rose, keys and a piece of paper with two words. "I'm sorry."

"It's perfect." Mrs. Miller came up with a huge grin. "That Jensen sure is a sweetheart. He told me he wanted to do something, for all you did for the movie crew and such."

"The…movie…oh, that's right." Cassie stuttered and opened the passenger door. She grabbed the note and put it into her pocket. "That was nice of…them."

"Oh, I'm sure it was all him." Mrs. Miller opened the back door and looked in. "This is perfect for your business."

Cassie rounded the vehicle once more and then walked toward the shop. She'd not let him do it, no way would she set herself up for disappointment when he pulled the Evil Jensen stunt.

Her phone buzzed as she walked back inside. It was Tesha. "Hey, girl." Cassie ensured her voice was light. "Are you in town?"

Tesha laughed. "Yes. I'm watching you from inside Jensen's car." She looked through the window to the Jaguar across the street. Her friend got out and Jensen drove away.

Mrs. Miller and Tesha hugged, and the older woman headed into the hardware store while Tesha crossed the street to hers. The bell jingled as her friend walked in. "Isn't it adorable?"

Tesha looked to the new SUV through the window. "I knew you were sold when you walked around it your hand never leaving it."

Cassie smiled at her friend. "I can't possibly keep it. It's too much."

Her friend rushed to her, her eyes wide. "Are you crazy? It's not that much to him. Besides, after losing you the Hollywood cupcake job, and the media mess, it's the least he could do."

So he'd not told Tesha about their night. Cassie let out a sigh of relief. "The media thing wasn't his fault. I suppose famous people can't have a personal life. Besides, I have to admit, it's helped business. The cupcake job, now that *was* his fault."

"Wanna share a cup of tea?" Tesha peered at the cupcake display with an expression of excitement. It would be lonely once Tesha left to move to Nashville. Cassie tried not to think of it, but the Tesha and Adam's wedding day was quickly approaching.

"How are the wedding plans going?" She placed a cup of tea on the counter and waited for Tesha to make up her mind on a cupcake.

Her friend gave an exaggerated eye roll. "Adam's mom is great. Only a few details left, and she insists on taking care of it. She and my mom are meeting with the caterer and going to the reception hall this week. They get along like long lost best friends."

"That leaves me out of much to do. Except plan a fun shower." Cassie leaned on the counter.

"No shower." Tesha shuddered. "They are boring. Let's just plan a girl's weekend away. Just you and me. I don't have any bridesmaids except Tristan's daughter."

"New York?"

Tesha gasped. "What a great idea!" She jumped up and down clapping. "Yes. That is perfect."

The SUV caught her attention. "It is a beautiful car. Subtle, not over the top and the logo on the back window is so adorable."

"You know…" Tesha's lips curved. "Adam says, Jensen only buys the family vehicles. He's given each of his brothers a car. So this means you're in. Part of the Ford clan now."

She let out a sigh. "I don't think that is the case. But it is a very nice gesture. Almost makes up for the loss of income from the cupcake job. He's still a butthead."

They laughed and Tesha pointed at an almond cupcake. "I want that one."

AN HOUR LATER, they arrived at Tesha's house. The setting sun gave the horizon a magical feel. The black Jag was parked at the house next door.

"Why is Jensen's car still there?" Cassie's stomach pitched. "I figured he'd be gone to Nashville by now."

Tesha shook her head. "No, he's staying here for a few weeks. Taking time off until the next movie or something like that."

"He's staying here in Lovely?" Her voice pitched and she groaned.

"Oh, stop," Tesha laughed. "You two can get along. You better make an effort at least to get through the wedding."

Of course Tesha was right. The last thing she needed to do was stress her out right now, with the wedding stuff coming up. "Sorry. I promise to be patient with him."

"And you will accept the car and thank him?" Her friend gave her a pointed look.

Cassie smiled. "I can't give it back. I'm in love with it." She patted the dashboard, and they got out and went into Tesha's house.

"What are you going to do with the place?" Cassie asked when they went inside.

Tesha put her purse down and went to the kitchen. She opened the refrigerator and took out some tea. "Debbie and Carol have been godsends. They're buying it. Partnering to open the B and B."

"That's awesome." Cassie accepted the glass of sweet tea. "They are filling in for me when I go to Nashville for your wedding preparation too. Of course, on the wedding day and the day after, I'll be closed for business."

The back door opened, and Jensen strolled in. He swaggered across the room, phone to his ear, before noticing them. "Oh, hey."

Since her new car was parked on the opposite side of the house, he didn't know she was there. His gaze went from them to the doorway, as if he wanted to escape.

"Hi Jensen," both replied in unison.

"What are you doing here?" he asked Tesha. "I thought you said you wanted me to check on the house." He slipped the phone into his back pocket.

"I meant later this week. I'm going to Nashville tomorrow." Tesha laughed. "I knew you weren't listening. Too busy watching Cassie and her new car."

Her heart thudded against her breastbone. The effect the man had on her was something between a heart attack and acid reflux.

She took a deep breath. "We should talk."

Jensen's gaze met hers and he shoved his hands into his front pockets. "Sure."

"Um…yeah, I need to water the plants." Tesha practically sprinted to the French doors and went outside.

Jensen stood next to the kitchen table, right next to where she sat. Cassie swallowed wanting to tell him to stay a good distance away. "I wasn't going to accept the car."

"Figured as much."

"But I can't give it back. It's great. A very nice gesture. Thank you very much."

"You're welcome."

Standing with his hands in his jean pockets, his wide shoulders stood out. His short answer made it harder to keep the conversation going, but it was time to say everything.

He bit his lip and frowned. She wondered if it was an expression from childhood. "I accept your apology," he said, his expression blank.

Cassie waited to see what he'd say.

"I can be rash and impulsive. I do things without thinking it through first. I talked to Caden, and he helped me see that what I do and say sometimes looks and sounds bad."

"It doesn't just look bad. Sometimes it is bad." Cassie put her glass down and closed the distance between them. "You asked Vanessa to not invite me to do the catering job in LA."

"That's because they are flighty. That was the third party they'd planned and canceled. I didn't want them to leave you hanging. You would have lost a lot of money if you'd bought plane tickets and all that only for them to call it off."

Cassie let out a breath. "And I'm a big girl and would have handled it if you would have told me what to expect."

"I didn't think about that." He lifted and lowered his shoulders "Sorry."

"You've already apologized. I'm the one that owes you an apology. No matter how mad you made me, I shouldn't have said the things I did at the hospital. It was wrong of me to say what I said. Please accept my apology."

He looked down at the floor. "Did you take the day after things?"

"What?" It took a minute to figure out what he meant, and her cheeks flushed. "No. I mean, I didn't even think about it."

His eyebrows rose and she placed her hand on his forearm. "I'm not pregnant." She removed her hand when the urge to move closer came over her.

"So…" she continued. "I'm so sorry for saying those mean things and for calling you a name."

"I can be an asshole." His lips curved.

"You didn't deserve for me to say those things. I was stressed."

Jensen moved to stand next to the kitchen counter. "So you and that guy work things out?"

She'd forgotten what she'd said about Nick. "Who? Oh no…he was and always will be my ex. He and I were engaged at one time."

"Wanna have dinner tomorrow night? I'll cook." His demeanor changed back to the carefree Jensen Ford. "I'll only accept your apology over my spaghetti Carbonara."

"I'm not sure that's a good idea. We have to get along until after the wedding. Spending time together is pushing it." She loved the idea of dinner with him, but at the same time didn't want to chance getting closer to him. It would be harder when he left.

"Friends have dinner. I think we can get along for one evening." He held his hand out. "Shake?"

"You are crazy." They shook hands and clapping sounded.

Tesha smiled broadly. "Yay. You are friends."

"At least for now," Cassie grumbled picking up her bag. "I gotta scoot. See you next week."

She hugged Tesha and waved at Jensen. "Dinner tomorrow."

Chapter Seventeen

IT WAS JUST dinner, a simple ritual that many people did every day without a second thought. A meal shared with a friend, Jensen repeated in his head, and checked the oven, releasing the wonderful aroma of his roasted chicken strips.

"Looking good, little buddies, just don't dry up."

Next he tossed the spaghetti, bacon and egg in a casserole dish and drizzled olive oil, minced garlic and seasoning over it. He put the dish onto the top oven rack to keep warm and began chopping a cucumber and a green pepper for the salad.

"That's right, it's just a meal. With a woman I happen to have it bad for," he grumbled out loud.

Part of him wished Cassie would not show up. It would make things easier. After all, she was not interested in pursuing a relationship with him. Not that he blamed her. Besides, with his schedule and his lifestyle, where would it leave her?

He'd considered it many times. Whoever he married would have to be very understanding, secure in their relationship and put up with his less than stellar personality. Then there were the fanatical fans. This was the familiar list he often repeated to himself when confirming it was best to remain a bachelor until he came back to Nashville and quit acting. He could afford it. Unlike many megastars, he didn't splurge on fancy houses or have any drug habits. His indulgence was spoiling the family. Cars for his brothers, vacations for his parents.

The doorbell buzzed and he let out a breath. "Don't say anything stupid," he reminded his mouth.

Cassie stood on the porch holding a bottle of wine and a bouquet of flowers. She thrust the flowers at him. "Apology flowers."

"Thanks." Jensen took them and stepped back allowing her through. "First time someone has given me flowers. They're…nice."

He stared at the colorful display. "Not sure where to put them. Adam doesn't have any vases."

Cassie took them back and gave him the wine. "I'll figure something out." She moved ahead of him to the kitchen. "Wow, it smells great. Did you pick whatever it is up at the diner?"

"I cooked."

"Really?" She whirled to face him. "You cooked?" It was nice to catch her off balance. Her pretty eyes shone with curiosity. "I didn't expect that."

"I told you I would. Mom taught us all to cook. Except for Tristan. He sucks at anything but grilling meat. Claims he doesn't like to cook."

She found a pitcher and filled it with water.

"Your Mom told me when I was over that all of you do well in the kitchen but that you were the best cook. Want to open the wine?"

It had been years since he'd been nervous on a date. Jensen uncorked the wine. "She did, huh? What else did she tell you about me?"

"That you wet the bed until you were ten."

"I did not." He realized by her trembling lips, she kidded him.

"Can you get a couple wine glasses?" The wine was a cabernet he'd not tried. Mostly he was a beer guy, rarely drank wine.

After he poured the wine, they both held the glasses up and Cassie touched hers to his. "To not fighting."

He sipped it and had to admit to liking the fruity dry taste. "It's good."

She climbed on a bar stool and watched him. "This is awesome. I get to drink wine and watch Mr. Movie Star cook."

The comment, although just conversation, unsettled him. It would be nice to just be a regular guy. Not someone who people saw as his work persona only.

"I'm just a guy, Cassie."

"I know." She drank from her glass, her eyes meeting his.

A few minutes later they sat at the table. It felt good to watch her enjoy his cooking. "If you ever get married, your wife will be lucky to have a hubby that can cook this good."

"Thanks." He cut a piece of chicken. "I like doing it."

"I assume you are a confirmed bachelor, with your career and all," Cassie said, between bites. "Probably good since it seems like most celebrity marriages don't last."

It was the opportunity he'd been waiting for. An opening to gauge how she felt about him. "I want to get married. Just have to find someone that is willing to put up with a lot." He chewed his meat and waited for what she'd say next.

"It shouldn't be hard. I mean…" She seemed discomfited.

"You've got a lot going for you and all."

Now he was curious. "Besides money, fame and this pretty mug? What else do I have?"

Her mouth opened and closed. "You have a good heart. A great family and are a giving person. And pretty good in…ummm…bed." She blushed and picked up her glass. "More wine?"

Jensen nodded.

"Yeah. I guess. Of course, most women don't look past the things I mentioned. So I can't trust that whoever I fall for really cares for me or the other stuff." He studied her expressions.

Cassie poured wine into his glass and met his gaze. "I suppose you're right." Her lips curved and his heart tumbled. "Love is hard anyway. I imagine it's tougher for you."

They talked about the town, keeping the rest of the conversation surface level as they finished eating.

She let out a contented sigh. "This was the best meal I've had in a long time. You are definitely a wonderful cook."

Warmth filled him. The compliment felt better than any profession recognition.

"I'm glad you liked it."

"Let's clean up the dishes. Then I need to head back. Got a lot to do before heading to Nashville on Thursday."

At the sink with her back to him, she ran the water. "I'll rinse them, you put them in the dishwasher."

Jensen chuckled. "You're kinda bossy." He came up behind her and kissed her jaw. "How about you sit down and let me do this."

"I..ummm." He kissed a bit lower on the side of her neck.

A soft gasp escaped, and she stepped sideways and faced him. "What are you doing?"

"A friendly smooch, that's all." He opened the dishwasher and began loading it. "Go sit down. Keep me company while I load these dishes, then I'll walk you to the door."

Her eyes narrowed, but she did as he asked.

THE KISS HAD rattled her. What was she doing there? Cassie knew she should be running out the door instead of sitting on a stool staring at the man's ass. He had nice butt. Filled out the jeans he wore quite nicely.

She took a fortifying breath. The thought of him marrying someone made her unsteady, and so jealous she wanted to throw something. The worst part was that with him being famous; whoever he dated would be splashed all over the television, and she'd have a hard time avoiding it.

"Jensen?"

He looked over his shoulder at her, his long-lashed eyes playful. "Yeah?"

"Why are you staying in Lovely? I thought you had another movie coming up."

The sound of the dishwasher coming to life was the only sound in the room. He walked around the counter and placed his hands on the counter, trapping her with his arms. "You."

"Me...what?" It was hard not to look at his lips, but looking into his eyes seemed even more intimate, so she looked from his eyes to the wall behind him. "Move back." Her hand on one of his shoulders, she pushed him away. He didn't budge.

"I want to spend more time with you. I want to get to know you better. See where things go."

It had to be a joke. He was up to something, and she wasn't about to play his game. On the other hand there was vulnerability in his eyes, she'd only seen once. When she'd insulted him at the hospital. "I don't know what to say."

"Are you willing to give me a chance? I want to be your man, Cassie."

"Oh." Her lips curved and eyes misted. At a loss for words, she touched his cheek. "I'm afraid."

"Me, too."

When his lips touched hers, it was the sweetest kiss she'd ever experienced. Their bodies remained separate. Only their mouths pressed together.

He pulled away and cupped her face holding it up and pressed a kiss to her forehead. "Give me a chance. That's all I ask."

What would happen after he left? If she gave in, her heart would be crushed into a million little pieces when he broke it. Jensen would be surrounded by beautiful women, skinny models, and made up, rich movie stars. Cassie wasn't sure she could withstand not being around him. Would jealousy make her too clingy? Most men hated clingy.

"What are you thinking?" He kissed her lightly and smiled. "I can see your wheels turning."

"I need to think. As much as I want to…be with you. I'm not sure I can be strong enough to be your girlfriend. What if I turn into a clingy sappy mess?"

He frowned and let out a long breath, his lips pressed into

a thin line, and he swallowed. "Then let's get married. Let's elope. You can be my clingy sappy wife."

"What? Are you crazy? We have to be at Adam and Tesha's wedding this coming weekend. I can't marry you without….umm….Is this some sort of gag?"

"No. Come here." He pulled her to her feet and wrapped his arms around her. She closed her eyes and leaned on him. In the embrace it was easy to say yes. Because it's where she wanted to remain. But why was he asking?

"I love you, Cassie. I don't want to lose you. Tell me what to do." His heart was beating fast and his breathing quicker than normal. "Talk to me."

She hugged him tight and then looked up at him. "You love me? But you don't even like me."

"I've been trying to keep you at arms length. Too damned scared to admit how I felt." He kissed her temple. "You're the one that doesn't like me."

"I like you. I more than like you. I'm totally in lust with you."

"That's good. It's a start." He chuckled. "Although I am hoping for more."

It became hard to breathe. To admit her feelings would leave her wide open, in the perfect position for him to tear her heart open. Love was about chances and maybe it was time she took another leap of faith.

He stepped back and she took his hand and put it up to her chest. His palm flattened above her breasts.

"You have my heart, Jensen. And right now the power to break it, because I am madly in love with you."

His eyes widened and his smile made her grin back at him.

"Hot damn!" Jensen grabbed her and lifted her off the floor, turning in a circle while laughing. "Yeah!"

"Put me down, you goof." Cassie was laughing, but with the combination of turning and the wine she'd drank, it made her dizzy.

Cassie slid down his body until her feet touched the ground, only to be kissed with so much force, she had to cling to him to keep from falling.

God help her, her life was about to change forever.

Chapter Eighteen

"It's been a busy day," Debbie said while icing cupcakes. "That bell over the door hasn't stopped dinging."

Cassie pulled a tray from the oven and began placing the tiny cakes onto a cooling rack. "Yes, the new tractor company is bringing more people to move here. The new subdivision is selling houses as quick as they're being built."

The night before, she'd left Jensen's house with so many mixed emotions, the entire drive home was a blur. Torn between grinning like a loon and "Oh God's" she'd barely slept. Despite the lack of sleep, the busyness of the day was helpful.

Customers walked in; a young mother and daughter moved to the display and Cassie went to help them. The bell over the door sounded again and a group of teens sauntered in.

What would happen to her cupcake shop if she married Jensen? What about Kayce? She didn't even know where he lived.

"Cassie?" Debbie gave her a puzzled look. "Isn't that your brother?"

One of the teens who'd walked in was Kayce. She'd not recognized him with the new buzzed hair. He grinned at her. "Hey, sis."

Moments later, she leaned back into the chair and stared at her brother. Her mind was awhirl.

"How could you do this? You joined the Air Force without discussing it with me."

Kayce shrugged. "I didn't want you to talk me out of it."

She choked back tears. "So you haven't been in school?"

"Nope, I was at boot camp. Heading to my next duty station next week."

"Duty station." Her mind was fuzzy, and she could only repeat words back at him. "Next week. How did you get away with being at book camp and me not knowing?"

Kayce grinned. "I told them you were special needs and needed to hear from me weekly. Then I told you I had to work every weekend."

"Smart ass." She sniffed into the tissue and wiped her eyes.

"Yep. Well, it's training school, anyway; I'll be there for six months. Going to be a computer geek. Then I'll get the follow-on assignment…."

Kayce continued talking. He was excited and motioned to his friends to join him. They'd driven from Florida and were planning to stay at her house overnight before heading back again for school. They explained plans and gave her all kinds of information that mostly flew over her head. Her baby brother was on his own. He was a man and from what she could decipher, graduated top of his class and had already been promoted.

"…Lakenheath, in the UK."

"You're going to England?" She finally was able to focus. "For what?"

Kayce patted her hand. "That's where I'm going to be stationed."

"Absolutely not, that is too far away." She felt faint. "I was planning to buy Tesha's truck for you. You need a vehicle, don't you?"

"Mom offered to buy me one. But I won't need one there," Kayce said and bit into a cupcake. "She said she feels bad that she didn't come to my graduation. She's acting different lately."

"So she knows you joined the Air Force then?" Cassie felt jealous that Kayce may have shared something with their mom first. Of course he probably should have, but that didn't affect her irrational proprietary feelings when it came to her brother.

Kayce grinned. "Nope, had to tell you first and let you break the news. I'm sure she'll be okay with it."

"I love you, Kayce."

Her brother leaned over and hugged her. "Thanks for everything, Sis. I love you too. Hey, is Jensen Ford still around? These guys don't believe me when I told them you're friends."

Oh boy.

THAT NIGHT, THE three boys ate pizza and watched college football, arguing over who'd win the game. Cassie sipped tea and looked down at the display on her phone. Jensen had asked to come over and she'd put him off, telling him about Kayce and his friends. Although the boys really wanted to meet the movie star, she wasn't ready to deal with that situation at the moment. To explain it to Kayce was something she was not prepared for. She wasn't sure what they were going to do yet. Jensen planned to remain in Lovely for four more weeks. That was barely enough time to get to know each other. Then he was flying to New Zealand to begin filming his next movie.

She eyeballed an unopened bottle of wine but decided against it. Hopefully, she'd get plenty of sleep tonight and get up early to fix Kayce and his friends a good farewell breakfast.

"Ding." On the display was another text from Jensen. *Tomorrow night. We'll talk. I'll be over.*

Maybe she'd not sleep. Her heart demanded that she say yes and give in to the wild adventure with Jensen Ford. Her brain had yet to get on board. How would she cope? Either way wouldn't be easy.

THE NEXT DAY, Cassie leaned on the counter at the shop, thankful for a small respite in customers. The shop was quiet after she turned off the radio when every love song irritated her more than the last. She let out a huff and pushed call on her cell phone. "Hello?" Her mother sounded relaxed. "Cassie?"

"Hey Mom. I called to tell you about Kayce."

"Did something happen?" Her mother's voice pitched, astounding Cassie. It was rare her mother showed any emotion when it came to her or her brother.

"He's fine. Joined the Air Force."

"Oh my goodness. I spoke to him several times, he never said anything."

"You called him?"

Her mother hesitated. "Yes, I missed him."

They talked for a few minutes, and she was pleasantly surprised. Usually her mother rushed her off the phone. Today it was as if they reconnected.

"Cassie?" Her mother paused. "Thank you for taking care of your brother. I haven't been there for him. Too busy trying to make things work with this man."

"Are you okay?" She wondered if yet another thing was about to jump onto her already overfilled mind.

"I'm great. Getting divorced." Her mother chuckled. "It's so different this time. I'm so happy. Relaxed and excited about making good changes. Maybe I can come there and help you with the cupcake shop. I love the idea of it. And it's so adorable. It's time for me to take care of me…"

They talked for another few minutes then her mother asked. "I saw the video. I sent you a text. Should have called to see if you were okay, but that was the same week I kicked Hank out."

"I'm glad you didn't call me. I am so embarrassed." She felt her cheeks heat.

"Oh, you shouldn't be, honey. That man is so darn cute. Looks like he's into you too. I hope things work out. That interview he did was so sweet."

"Interview?"

"Yes, on the The Late Show with Stephen Colbert. Didn't you see it?" Her mother gushed. "Let me know if you and Jensen Ford are going to give it a go, so I can start bragging."

They hung up and Cassie rushed to her small office and wiggled the mouse to wake up her computer. She went directly to YouTube and typed, "Jensen Ford interview on Stephen Colbert."

She stared at the still shot once the video ended, only moving when the bell over the door sounded.

THE EVENING WAS perfect, the light breeze coming through her open patio door freshened the house. Her hand trembled slightly when she lit a candle and placed it on her small dining room table. She pushed her hair behind an ear and looked at the clock once again.

Seven thirty. Jensen was already half an hour late. If he didn't show up, she wouldn't be surprised. After all, what else did she expect? For a movie star like him to actually want to date her? What he'd said on the television show, although sweet, may have all been an act.

"I can see your wheels turning." Jensen stood at the patio door. He smiled at her.

Cassie blinked at him. "Why did you come in through the back?"

"When I rode up the side road I saw you out here." He walked in and went directly to her. Immediately she went into his embrace, needing the assurance he really was there. Jensen chuckled. "I missed you, too."

Whatever cologne he wore was intoxicating and Cassie buried her face into his neck. "You smell so good."

"Good to know." He held her tight. "I was afraid you'd call and cancel. Then when my agent called and I couldn't get him off the damned phone, I was hoping you wouldn't be too mad to open the door."

He took her mouth then and walked her backward to the bedroom. At once both tore at each other's clothing, not able to stop. Shirts, pants, shoes and everything else were done away with in record time.

The roughness of his hands on her skin made each caress feel like fire on her already sensitive skin. She arched into his touch while running her own over his body, enjoying the hills and valleys of each muscular inch. When he rose over her and looked down at her, she could see love in his gaze. He smiled down at her and then took her nipple between his lips. Cassie could barely breathe; she was drowning in him and didn't care.

He trailed his tongue down between her breasts and she closed her eyes while running her fingers through his hair. "Oh, Jensen."

"Mmmm?" He'd reached the apex between her legs, and he pushed her legs apart. "You're perfect, Cassie."

The heat of his mouth taking her sex in made her cry out. Each nip and flick of his tongue took her higher until she began to shake. Jensen was relentless, didn't slow until she came with force.

While she still quaked from the release, he settled between her legs and took himself in hand and guided to her entrance.

"Condom." Cassie held his hips to keep him from moving further.

"Got it covered." Jensen took her hand and brought it to touch him. His hardness was indeed sheathed.

When he thrust into her, once again she became lost in the sensations. Not wanting to miss anything, she watched Jensen moving over her. He was perfect, his eyes closed, lips parted as he made love to her. With each movement he took them higher. Finally Cassie could not stop herself from wrapping her legs around his hips and urging him to move faster, take her harder.

Her hand slid down his slick back and she cupped his butt, bringing him deeper.

"I want you so much. Don't want tonight to end." His husky voice in her ear as sensual as his movements. "Damn, you feel so good." Jensen's breathing hitched.

With a primal groan Cassie let go, no longer able to keep up with him. The climax hit her hard and all control was lost. In the whirlwind of sensations, she heard Jensen's deep moan as he, too came.

"THAT WAS AMAZING." She opened her eyes and looked to Jensen, who lay on his back, breathing hard.

He grinned. "I think three times is a record for me."

Cassie pulled the blankets up over them. "I need to get some sleep. Need to be at the shop in the morning." Once covered she snuggled closer to him and lay her head on his chest. "You okay?"

His arms surrounded her, and he pressed a kiss to her temple. "We haven't talked yet. I'm hungry."

It was two o'clock in the morning and they sat cross-legged on the bed eating grilled cheese sandwiches and tortilla chips. Cassie reached for her glass of water and drank deeply. "This has to be the best grilled cheese I've ever had."

The mood changed when Jensen let out a breath. "You're not going to marry me, are you?" At his forlorn expression she couldn't help touching his face.

"What makes you think that?"

He shrugged and picked at his sandwich. "Because before I could start this conversation we ended up making love."

Cassie tried not to laugh. "We end up making love because you're so damn sexy."

Once again he sighed. "Whatever."

"Look…" She put her plate on the nightstand and went closer to him. "Jensen."

He straightened, seemed to be fortifying himself for her to turn him down. Of course, he'd read her right. To keep from talking, she'd been putting it off. How could she marry him? The idea terrified her.

"I am scared to death of marrying you. I'm sorry, but I am."

"I understand." He pushed his plate away. "Don't blame you."

"But." She moved closer and kissed his lips. "I'm even more frightened of being apart from you. So…" she gulped in air to her lungs that felt as if collapsing. "Let's do it. Let's elope. I don't want time to change my mind."

His face split into a grin and he threw her onto the bed and fell over her. "You said yes! I can't believe you said yes."

"We're not doing it again." Cassie laughed. "We need sleep."

He kissed her and reached for the lamp. In minutes the room was dark.

Cassie sighed. "Sleep is overrated."

Chapter Nineteen

"YOU GOT MARRIED?" Miriam Ford cried out.

Cassie braced herself for the Ford family's reaction to the news. Right after leaving the courthouse, they'd gone directly to Nashville.

The entire way she'd picked at her nails until they were a bloody mangled mess.

Jensen on the other hand was calm and chatty. From what they'd do for the next three weeks, to traveling to New Zealand, he wanted to discuss every detail. So much so that Cassie had finally given in and pulled up her phone calendar so they could get specific dates. When they'd turned into the Ford's driveway, she'd almost hyperventilated from nerves.

It was only his steady hand on the small of her back that kept her from bolting into the woods behind the property and hiding.

"Oh my goodness!" Jensen's mother hugged her and kissed both cheeks. "This is wonderful."

Even after Jensen's father pulled her into a bear hug, Cassie could barely form a cohesive thought.

Tesha rushed to her and jumped up and down. "I knew it!" she screamed and did a little dance. "I knew it. I knew it."

"What do you mean?" Cassie was actually shocked that her friend had not said anything to her about her suspicions.

"That Jensen was in love with you and you with him. The chemistry between you two was off the charts." Tesha wiped a tear away. "I'm so happy. We're sisters!"

Jensen's mother laughed. "Caden told me Jensen was in love and we suspected it was you. I had been praying he didn't fall for one of those Hollywood types, but someone like you. One of us regular people."

"I'm going to cry now." Tears were already spilling, and Cassie sniffed. Jensen placed his arm around her and pulled her close.

They all moved to the living room and Tesha insisted they tell her what happened after she left. Leaving out all the sex was hard, but they managed to give the PG rated version. Roman Ford poured champagne for the five of them.

"What's going on?" Tristan, Jensen's eldest brother, walked into the room. It was the first time Cassie had seen him in many days.

His dark blue eyes took her in, but he didn't smile. Instead he looked to his mother. "Celebrating?"

"Oh honey, you won't believe what Jensen did." Miriam seemed not to notice her son's austerity. "Jensen married Cassie. They eloped today."

It was endearing to see Tristan go to Jensen and hug him so tightly. "Good for you. I love you," Tristan told Jensen, who smiled at his brother.

"Back at ya, bro."

A sixth glass was poured and given to Tristan. They toasted. And once again Cassie had to wipe away tears.

"I'm not usually a crier. I promise," she told no one in particular.

"Can we not cook today?" Jensen asked his mom. "How about we order Chinese?"

"Good idea." His mother looked to Cassie. "When the boys were young, we were celebrating they'd all gotten good grades one day. I made a big deal out of making a special dinner and I got distracted and it all burned up. So we ended up ordering Chinese. It's sort of a family tradition now. When something special happens we order Chinese."

"Perfect," Cassie replied, laughing. "I love it."

The family moved to sit around the kitchen table just as Adam and Caden entered. They were filled in and once again, hugs were exchanged. Caden was assisted to sit, although he argued the whole time.

"So excited that we're sisters now," Tesha whispered to Cassie. "And part of this wonderful family."

Cassie exchanged looks with Jensen, who winked at her from where he stood amongst his brothers. "I'm home. I'm finally, truly, home."

The doorbell rang.

"Food's here." Tristan went to get the door while Jensen and Adam began pulling out plates and silverware. Their mother directed them to get glasses refilled from the table.

She gave Cassie a sheepish smile. "I've got them trained for you two. Don't let them get away with not helping around the house."

Both she and Tesha leaned back in their chairs. "Yes, ma'am."

Epilogue

ADAM, TRISTAN AND Jensen made a stunning picture at the front of the chapel.

Cassie made her way up the aisle behind Nahla, who wore a beautiful pink dress. Her dress was chocolate brown. The scent of flowers wafted through the air along with the harp music.

She stood next to Nahla and faced the back of the church. Tesha was a vision in a white mermaid dress. With a long veil that hung to the floor from the back of her hair and holding bunch of white and pink roses, she was stunning.

The bride's eyes were locked with her soon-to-be husband's. When Cassie stole a glance toward Adam, her breath caught. A single tear trailed down his face and he smiled broadly, deep dimples showing.

Her own breath caught, and she looked to Jensen, who watched her. He mouthed, "I love you." And she swallowed and blinked to keep from turning into a blubbering mess.

THE RECEPTION WAS magical. It was outdoors in a beautiful botanical garden. Lights were strung throughout, giving the impression of twinkling stars. Between watching the bride and groom dance in their own world and Nahla coaxing her father to dance with her.

Cassie was having the time of her life, dancing, drinking and tasting all the delicious appetizers.

Her mother looked pretty, her blonde hair up in a French twist. She was moving to Lovely, to take over Sweet Indulgence, and was quite excited at the prospect. Cassie was cautiously optimistic, but hopeful, at her mother's new start.

She leaned into her husband's embrace when he pulled her into the dance floor. "Our first dance," Cassie beamed up at him as they swayed to Adele's Love Song.

"It's a good one too. Perfect for us." He looked into her eyes and repeated a line from the song. "You make me whole again."

Just as she was about to tell him it was a corny line, he dipped her, and she let out a peal of laughter.

FROM HIS SEAT at a table, Caden looked on and couldn't help the warmth that flowed through him. His parents swayed to the music, their gazes locked. Adam's carefree expression was like the brother, he'd not seen since before he'd gone to war.

Most surprising of all was Jensen's surprise marriage. It was obvious his brother was in deep, barely able to keep from his new bride.

Even his morose eldest brother Tristan was enjoying himself, he'd tossed off his suit jacket and had been dancing with Nahla and every aunt present.

Life was good for the Ford family.

He'd ensure it remained that way. Already he'd threatened Patrick to keep his secret. The fact that numbness was crawling up his right leg. That he couldn't move it without using his hands.

The following week, he'd meet with a specialist. If what he suspected was right, he'd never be able to return to his official duties. His life was about to take a turn that he wasn't sure he was prepared for.

Nobody's Hero… Caden's Story.

About the Author

Hello Dear Reader,

I love hearing from you and am always excited when you join my newsletter to get a free book and to keep abreast of new releases and other things happening in my world. Newsletter sign up: https://goo.gl/jLzPTA

USA Today Bestselling author Hildie McQueen pens captivating romances. The heroes are alpha males, the heroines are fiery, resilient women. You'll love the passionate romance and captivating action under a canopy of beautiful settings.

Her favorite past-times are traveling, reading and discovering tiny boutiques. She resides in a beautiful Georgia small-town with her super-hero husband Kurt, and three little dogs.

Website: www.HildieMcQueen.com
Facebook: facebook.com/HildieMcQueen
Email: Hildie@HildieMcQueen.com

Keep Calm and Read On!!

Printed in Great Britain
by Amazon